SHARON A. MITCHELL

TRUST

VINCI

BOOKS

By Sharon A. Mitchell

When Bad Things Happen

Vinci Books

vinci-books.com

Published by Vinci Books Ltd in 2025

1

The EU GPSR authorised representative is Logos Europe, 9 rue Nicolas
Poussion, 17000 La Rochelle, France
contact@logoseurope.eu

Prologue

"Look at me, Timothy. Look at mommy." Elizabeth watched her son closely, watching for any sign that he heard her or even noticed her presence. She lowered herself further, trying to put her face directly in front of his.

Timothy turned his head to avoid her, intent on the object he'd sent spinning. His gaze intent, his concentration never swerving.

Elizabeth sat back on her heels and sighed. She closed her eyes and tilted her face upwards, willing the tears not to fall. How could she feel this way about her son, her only child? She loved him with fierce determination and would lay down her life for him in an instant. She had proved that just a month ago. But this overwhelming love was shadowed by such frustration.

After surviving their ordeal, she had thought that she and Timothy would be closer than ever. After all, it was just the two of them now, two against the world, making their way together. She would keep him safe at all costs this time.

Steeling her determination to connect with this little

man, Elizabeth tried again. With babies, she'd read how you should have tummy time, when you would both lay on the floor together playing and examining objects. As the child became a toddler, that changed to floor time, where you'd sit on the floor and play together.

Timothy had no problems playing on the floor; in fact, that was how he preferred to spend his time these days. The problem was that that play time did not include her. Her little boy did not seem to need her, to want her.

Reaching into the bottom drawer for another pot lid, Elizabeth tried to mimic her son's actions. She set the lid carefully on its side and, with the thumb and first two fingers of her right hand, gave it a spin. The lid twirled nicely in a circle once, twice, then wobbled as its arcs became erratic and started to topple.

Timothy's hand shot out and caught it before it touched the floor. Moving it out of his mother's reach, he set it in perfect, practiced spin. He angled his body away from his mom and set a third pot lid spinning.

Trying not to feel the sting of rejection, Elizabeth rose to make herself a cup of tea. She needed to do something with her hands, something to push back the hurt.

Life had not gone the way she'd expected this last while. Who could have guessed what her life would become? But throughout it all, despite it all, the one thing she had never imagined was that this distance between her and her only child would grow.

Chapter One

"Come on, Timothy. Hurry up. We don't want to be late for Dr. Muller." Elizabeth threw back her head and let out a breath. Now she'd blown it. She'd said the two words guaranteed to make her son balk - hurry and late. It never failed.

Elizabeth hated being late. Absolutely hated it. Growing up, tardiness had been a strict no-no. It showed a lack of respect for other people's time. It presented you as a disorganized person, someone not in control of themselves. That would never do for a properly brought up young lady. Ah, she missed her parents.

Forcing herself to relax her shoulders, take two deep breaths, and paste a smile on her face, she got down to her son's level. "Timothy, Dr. Muller is waiting for us. You know how much you like going to his office. He has that wooden train you can play with."

That got her son's attention. He adored that train on the colorful wooden tracks. No matter how long they might have to sit in the waiting room, as long as he could push that train in its endless loop, he was content.

Mid-morning traffic was light. She planned her appointments that way, especially now since she no longer took the direct, predictable route to the doctor's office, or to anywhere else for that matter. No more distracted driving for her. Elizabeth's eyes scanned the road in front, through the rear-view mirror and both sides constantly, watching for anything out of the ordinary, any sign of danger. You could never be too careful. She knew that only too well.

Pulling into the parking lot behind the office, she kept her hands on the steering wheel, the engine running, and the doors locked as she surveyed the lot. A mom and two small children left the building, heading for an SUV. A man carrying a briefcase hurried from a BMW to the back door, his head down, one hand working his phone. He did not glance in her direction.

Assured that no one had her in their sights, Elizabeth chided herself for her paranoia. But is it really paranoia when someone is actually out to get you? No, she reminded herself. We're safe now. The culprits had been caught and the bad stuff could never happen again.

Sure, tell that to my pounding heart, she told herself.

Pasting on that fake smile she feared she was perfecting, Elizabeth looped the strap of her purse over her head and across one shoulder. This kept both of her hands free. She got out of the car, taking another careful look around the vicinity. Somewhat reassured that there was no one around who meant them harm, she opened the back door. Leaning in, she undid Timothy's seatbelt. Before helping him from the car, she again checked that no one was paying them undue attention.

Thankful for the parking space so close to the entrance, she pressed the button to lock her car doors and set the alarm.

Seeing Dr. Muller felt like meeting up with an old friend. Pitiful, Elizabeth thought, that your son's doctor was almost your only friend. Still, she trusted him and extended that trust to very few people.

Pulling the journal from her purse, she offered it to the doctor. As a pediatric neurologist, Dr. Peter Muller saw all sorts of parents. Elizabeth was one of his favorites. Her dedication to her son was obvious. Plus, she followed his instructions, intelligently weighing options, reporting side effects, and partnering in Timothy's care. It wasn't always like that.

The journal recorded everything that Timothy had eaten over the last two weeks, the time and dose of each medication, any possible reactions, and data about how he spent his time, his responsiveness, developmental milestones, and any verbalizations. Of most pressing concern were the records of seizure activity.

Timothy's seizures were not under control. They were working on that or had been before the kidnapping. Being off his meds for almost a week had taken a toll on his small body, and his seizure activity increased. They were getting them back under control. Perusing Elizabeth's notes, Dr. Muller smiled.

"Good, good," he said. "We're nearly back on track, aren't we?"

"Yes, or getting there. There's been no tonic-clonic seizures since, well, since we got home and back on these meds. The absence seizures are lessening, too, or at least that I've noticed those small moments where he seems to freeze, then comes back."

"I see that. Good. Don't beat yourself up about noticing them. Some happen briefly and no one, not even the best mom in the world has her eyes on her child one hundred percent of the time." He smiled. "And I'm including you among the best moms."

"Right. A mom that allows her child to get kidnapped and go without life-sustaining medications."

"We've been through this before. You cannot continue to blame yourself for things that were beyond your control. You held up admirably and you and your little man are safe, mainly thanks to your efforts."

Elizabeth gave a half-smile. "Thanks. It's just hard, you know. So many what-ifs run through my mind."

"Understandable."

Elizabeth's one shoulder raised, then lowered.

"How are *you* sleeping?" Dr. Muller's gaze searched hers.

"Me? I'm fine," she assured him quickly. "I think that Timothy is sleeping better now. I'm not sure, but I think that since we started this ketogenic diet, he sleeps through the night."

"Yes, other parents remark on that, as well. While this diet isn't the first thing that we try with one so young, for some kids with intractable seizures, it can be worth a try, at least until we get things settled down.

"But, back to you," he continued. "How are *you* doing?"

"I'm focusing on Timothy these days and on trying to get our lives back to normal. I'm working on getting us into a routine, one that's calm and predictable."

"You deserve some time to veg out and regroup. Everything you've been through would throw someone not as strong as you into a tailspin."

"Strong? No. We wouldn't have been in that position if I were strong."

"Nonsense. But that kind of talk isn't helpful. Have you

thought more about my suggestions of counseling you and for some form of play therapy for Timothy?"

Elizabeth shifted in her seat. "Not really. Things are still all so new, and I feel like we're in recovery mode."

Dr. Muller nodded. "Understandable. You *are* in recovery mode and will be for some time. That's why a good counselor would be helpful. You'll need help in figuring out how to move on from this. Even though you're safe now, the trauma remains imprinted in your mind. You need help in dealing with it."

She shrugged. "Maybe." She smiled up at him. "I don't mean to seem ungrateful, and I appreciate your concern. But I only seem to have so much energy right now, and it is all directed at Timothy and helping him to get better.

"I wanted to ask you about something else." She checked to see that the train held Timothy engrossed. "I'm worried. Yes, the seizures are better, but there are other changes in him since, well, since we got back home." She checked again, but her son ran the train along the floor along a track that only he could see. "I've lost him." Tears smarted her eyes. "He's here with me, but it feels like he isn't. There was a time when we were close, almost like any mother and son. I know that he has never been the most affectionate child, and he's always happily done his own thing. I used to be proud of the way he could amuse himself for hours. But lately, it's almost as if he doesn't need me, doesn't see me. He's content by himself and doesn't seem to want me to enter into his world." Now the tears came. She hastily turned her face; Timothy should not see her like this.

Dr. Muller handed over a box of tissues gave her a minute to get herself under control. "And you think that this has increased since your ordeal?"

She nodded.

"Have you considered that this might be a reaction to what the two of you went through? His way of processing events that would be hard for an adult to understand, let alone a preschooler, and one with limited language skills?"

"I've thought of all kinds of things, including that this is his way of punishing me for letting so many bad things happen to us."

"He's four, Elizabeth. That's a pretty elaborate punishment plan for a small child to concoct and maintain, don't you think?"

"Yes." She gave a half-smile. "I only think that when I'm feeling, well, you know."

Elizabeth's lips formed a firm line. She shook her head. "I can't bear the thought of strangers around Timothy." She held up her hand. "Not even professionals recommended by *you*."

Dr. Muller waited.

"Maybe one day, I'll be ready," Elizabeth continued. Then I'll think about counseling. But for now, I want to get used to life with just the two of us. That's our reality, so we'd better get comfortable with it. We're all each other needs."

Chapter Two

A knock. Elizabeth's eyes darted to the front door, reassured when she saw that the deadbolt was in place. Although how could it not be when she must check it dozens of times a day?

The knock came again. Maybe if she ignored it, whoever would go away. For weeks the press hounded them, but she thought that she, Timothy, and her husband Jackson had become yesterday's news. Still, you never knew when a lone reporter would try to make a name for himself.

She turned on the outside security camera. The grainy picture showed a woman, turned away from the door and laughing at someone out of the lens' range. She looked vaguely familiar, maybe a newscaster she'd seen on television.

The woman turned toward the door and rang the bell. Now she recognized her - a neighbor.

They had the sort of neighbors whom you would nod politely in passing or wave a hand to when driving by. Pleasant, but they didn't really know any of them. Jackson, well, Jackson worked a lot and was rarely home. At least, that's what Elizabeth used to *believe* he was doing.

The woman wasn't giving up. She leaned into the doorbell and raised and lowered the door knocker repeatedly. What was up with her? Could she not take a hint?

"Elizabeth, I know that you're in there. I saw when your car drove up. It's me, Cynthia, your neighbor. I'll just take a minute of your time." She waited. When there was nothing, she added, "I know that you must be gun-shy with the press. Believe me, I'm alone and have nothing to do with those vultures. Just give me a couple minutes, please. I'm on your side and want to help."

Elizabeth had had it with trusting that people were supposedly on her side. Look where that had got her - almost dead. But this woman wasn't going away. Nothing she'd yelled through the door was worthy of calling the police. Besides, she was just a little woman; Elizabeth could probably take her in a fight. *Now where had that come from? She, Elizabeth Whitmore in a fight? Her mother would roll over in her grave.* She grinned to herself.

Anyone who could bring a smile to her face these days deserved a few seconds of her time. Raising her voice, she hollered, "Coming", as if she'd been at the back of the house. *Imagine me yelling. Oh, my poor mother would faint dead away at such unbecoming behavior.*

She smoothed her hair back, then opened both deadbolts, then the latch. She left the screen door closed and locked. Pasting on her best prep-school girl smile, she greeted her neighbor.

"Hi! I'm Cynthia from next door." She pointed over her left shoulder. "I'm not sure you remember me. I introduced myself when we first moved in. Cynthia Blythe." She held out her right and used her left to try to open the screen door. It didn't budge.

Looking over her shoulder to make sure that Timothy had not come downstairs, Elizabeth unlatched the door and stepped out onto the step. "Hello. I'm Elizabeth Whitmore. It's nice to meet you again." She gave the woman's hand a delicate, quick squeeze.

"You have my deepest sympathies for everything that you and your son have been through. You have my admiration, and I'm so glad that you're all right. We were so worried when we heard on the news that you were missing."

"Thank you. We're fine now."

That last bit gave Cynthia pause. "Yes. Well, I'm sure you are, but it will take some getting over."

Elizabeth gave her formal smile. Her mother's words rang in her head - "Keep yourself to yourself." Apt advice. Look what letting others in had led to.

Cynthia's smile faltered just slightly, but she plowed on. "Look. I understand." At Elizabeth's look, she stopped. "Well, no, I don't, really. No one could unless they've been through the exact same thing. But I'd like to understand, and I'd like to help."

"Thank you, but we're fine."

For a small woman, Cynthia had some bulldog tendencies. "I've been watching. No, I'm not a noisy neighbor, just concerned. Once I called the police when those reporters tried looking in your windows when you weren't home. A few times I drove them off with threats of reporting them." At Elizabeth's look, she hurried on. "No, I didn't talk to them. Ever. Sure, they tried asking me questions about you and your husband, but I never answered them, not once. I wouldn't do that.

"I get what it's like when strangers are intrusive. Believe

me, I know. I also get that feeling, that preservation instinct that tells you to just cocoon at home with your child. I also know that that can't continue forever. Sometimes you need to let someone else in, to let them help." She took a big breath and continued nervously. "I'm a private person, too. Really. And, before this I would not have dreamed of pushing myself on you. But you need help, and from the look of the amount of company you've had lately, I think you could use a friend."

"Thank you, but we are quite all right on our own. Thank you for coming over." Elizabeth opened the door and was halfway inside when she heard something.

She and Cynthia turned at the squeal and giggle that came from Elizabeth's front yard.

"Amy, I told you to stay on our grass."

The little girl raced around the lawn, followed by and following a grinning ball of fluff with a tail that looked like it was about to wag right off. The child and dog rolled on the ground together, making it hard to tell which of the two was the most energetic.

Cynthia turned back to Elizabeth. "Sorry about that." She waved a hand toward the duo. "My daughter Amy and Blitz, her dog. Blitz is over a year old now, but you'd think she was still a pup."

There was noise behind her, and Elizabeth turned to see that her son had entered the foyer. She let out an unladylike squeal as something furry brushed by her shins and attacked Timothy. He tumbled to the ground with the squirming bundle of white fluff in his arms his face bathed with who knows what sort of doggie breath. Thank god those sounds coming from the canine weren't snarls, but yips of what seemed to be welcome.

And what was that other noise? Giggles! Actual giggles

coming from her son's throat. When was the last time she heard such a thing?

The door pushed open behind her, and the little girl from next door jumped into the fray, rolling and laughing with Timothy and Blitz.

"I'm so sorry. Here, let me separate these monsters and get them out of your house." Cynthia's flush started at her cheeks and filled all the skin down to her collarbones.

Elizabeth's shock receded and her mama bear instinct rose. While she knew that Timothy was not being harmed by either the dog or the little girl, he had allergies. Likely. They didn't know for sure yet, but he might have all sorts of allergies. She knew that many kids reacted to cat and dog dander, but since her son had never been close to animals, she didn't know if he would have a reaction. Any sort of reaction could bring on a seizure.

Cynthia took a leap and her right foot landed on a dangling dog leash. "Got ya." She dragged the dog off of the children. "If you don't mind, I'll just tie him out here to your railing." Without waiting for permission, she left, secured the dog to the front step, then let herself back inside. As Cynthia brushed by, and toed off her sneakers, Elizabeth glanced down, noticing the perfect dog print on one of her own cream suede shoes.

In that brief time, Amy had spied Timothy's wooden blocks scattered about the living room floor. "Cool," she said, as she darted into the room. "Wanna play?"

Timothy sat down several feet away from this strange girl and watched as she began building, chattering non-stop the whole time.

"She'll rarely let him get a word in. She's my little chatterbox."

"Timothy doesn't say much." Elizabeth watched as

Timothy followed Amy's lead and attached wheels to a larger block.

"Looks like they'll be entertained for a while."

A while? Did they think that they'd been invited in?

Chapter Three

Cynthia awkwardly balanced the china teacup between her thumb and index finger. It clattered when she placed it onto its saucer. "Sorry. I'm more used to mugs, I guess."

Elizabeth nodded. While courtesy required that she offer tea or coffee, she was not prepared to be besties with anyone, and that included her neighbor. They would have a civilized cup of tea, then go back to the nodding acquaintance they'd enjoyed for the past few years.

Cynthia had other ideas. "I've been following your case on the news."

Elizabeth stiffened. Although she tried to keep her facial expression passive, her eyes gave her away.

Cynthia raised both hands. "Sorry. I'm not trying to be nosy. Honestly! Yeah, I know more about you than you know about me; your life is news.

"That's why I came over today. *Your* life may be news, and people all over are paying attention, but you might not want Timothy to hear it all. I know that the two of you have been going to the trial most days. It's mentioned in the news reports on the court case's progress.

"Soon, the parts about his father will come up." She pointed in the living room's direction, where they could hear Amy's almost non-stop voice. "Things will be discussed there, and accusations made about your husband that you might not want Timothy to hear."

There was a fine line between aloof and haughty and Elizabeth had perfected it. "I can watch out for my son on my own, thank you. He will be fine; I will take care of him."

"Of course, you will. But there will be times when you must testify. You'll be up front in the courtroom and Timothy cannot be with you. You wouldn't want him to hear some of that, anyway."

The judge, the social worker and now this noisy neighbor - all people trying to insert themselves into her life - hers and Timothy's.

But Cynthia echoed worries that plagued Elizabeth's mind, worries that she'd shoved deep and labelled as things to think about down the road. That day was not here yet, but was coming up. Soon.

"The reason I came over was to offer to watch Timothy sometimes while you're in court. Amy and I are almost always home, and as you see, the kids get along great."

"Thank you for your offer, but Timothy and I are a team. Where I go, he goes. I need him with me, and we stick together.

"And now, it's time for his nap." She rose. "I'll see you out."

Another knock. Since they'd lived here, they could go weeks

without someone rapping on their door. So now, just when she wanted to be left alone, it becomes a daily occurrence?

Elizabeth turned on the outdoor cameras. All but one showed no one. She watched for a few moments to be sure the man at the door didn't have an accomplice lurking somewhere around her property. Assured that the rest of the yard was clear, she turned her attention to the screen that showed the front door. As the man's profile turned towards the lens, her breath caught. What was *he* doing here? She'd not seen Detective Jake Dean since they'd been rescued in that hotel room. The door knocker sounded again.

Surely, he wasn't here to warn her of some new threat. Lord love a duck. How many people could there be who were out to get her? Wasn't five of them enough, all behind bars now?

She pressed the speaker. "Mr. Dean. How may I help you?"

"Good day, Ms. Whitmore. I wasn't sure if you'd remember me."

"I'd hardly forget many moments of that day." She altered her tone. "Thank you again for coming to our aid."

"You're welcome. Just doing my job." He shifted his feet. "May I come in and speak to you for a few moments?"

Elizabeth debated. She really did not want to have to deal with anyone right now. She couldn't seem to throw off the exhaustion that had settled on her shoulders and focusing on herself and Timothy was the max effort she could put in on these non-trial days. But he might have important news. Talking through the door suited her, but she owed this man more courtesy than that.

"Just a minute, please." She undid first the top deadbolt,

then the lower one, before releasing the lock in the door-knob and opening the main door.

Jake went for the screen door's handle, but it was locked.

As Elizabeth released the final lock and stepped back, he pulled open the screen and entered the foyer, brushing his shoes on the mat.

He held out his hand. "I wanted to check up on you, to see how you and Timothy are doing."

"Is that part of your normal duties?"

"Sometimes." His grin was sheepish. "Well, not often, although we'd like to have the time to do more follow-up." He trailed Elizabeth into the living room.

Elizabeth's head came up, wary. Anything out of the ordinary worried her these days.

Jake held up his hands. "No, no, there's nothing wrong or nothing new with the case." He rubbed the back of his head. "It's just that you and your son have stuck in my mind. You went through more in a week than most people suffer in a lifetime. My partner, Brendan, wanted to come, too, but he got tied up at work, and couldn't get away. But he'll be by sometime."

They sat in the living room and he continued. "I have a soft spot for kids." He amended that. "I never used to think much about them until I was posted to schools as a liaison officer. Then I became involved with a single mom and her son - my girlfriend and her little boy. Daniel is the same age as your Timothy. I keep thinking that if it had been Keira going through your ordeal, I'd really like for her to have a friend. Some friends."

When there was no reply, he added, "Keira's like you - she's tough."

He sees me as tough, Elizabeth thought. He's probably

the first person in my life to ever put that word together in the same sentence as me.

"Tough on the outside, at least," Jake continued. "She's had to be. I admire that kind of grit."

"People do what they have to do at the time." No biggie. When the life of your child is at stake, there's no choice.

"Not true. In my line of work, I see all sorts of reactions to adversity." He glanced around, seeing signs that a child lived there, but no Timothy. "How is the little guy?"

"He's fine, thank you." Her primly folded hands didn't fidget. That's not what a lady did. She forced herself to sit back.

Jake regarded Elizabeth. Something about her reminded him of his Keira. His. Funny how he was starting to think of her that way. And Daniel. He brought himself back to the woman in front of him. She didn't look open to a heart-to-heart. That's a relief. Touchy-feely wasn't his thing, either; he was a man of action, of doing and letting the feelings work themselves out. "I thought that Timothy might enjoy a playmate. Maybe I could bring Keira and Daniel by sometime and let the boys get together."

Elizabeth's default reaction was obvious. No. Hell, no, Jake thought, if he was reading her correctly. Well. He'd gotten through Keira's defenses and if he could do that, this woman's guard should be easy.

"I thought that Timothy could use a friend."

"He has me," assured Elizabeth. "That's all he needs for now." She'd worry about more later.

"Sometimes just playing with another kid can get his mind off things rather that dwelling on the bad that happened."

"My son does not dwell. He plays fine here, by himself

and with me." That latter bit was perhaps a stretch, but in time, it would be true. True enough for this man, anyway.

Jake rubbed his hands up and down his thighs and stood up. "Well, thanks for your time and I'm glad that you're doing all right." He walked to the door, turning with one hand on the knob. "I'll be back again and maybe bringing Keira and Daniel with me next time." Before she could protest, he added, "Just for a little play." He shut the door behind him before she could say more.

Yeah, right, thought Elizabeth as she engaged the door locks. Like that is ever going to happen.

Chapter Four

"All rise."

Elizabeth reached for Timothy's hand to help him to his feet. He pulled his hand away, grasping tightly to his Etch-a-Sketch. She settled for guiding him with his arm instead.

Once they were seated, his toy again captured Timothy's concentration. The dexterity he showed with it amazed his mother. She was sure that at age ten she would not have been as skilled with it as was this four-year-old boy. Books she read talked about preschool boys having weaker fine motor skills than girls of the same age, but she doubted that was true for Timothy.

She pulled her attention back to the courtroom, relieved that Timothy would zone out, paying little heed to what was going on around him, absorbed in his Etch-a-Sketch. Good thing, since they were spending so much time in this room.

Judge Bursey began. This week's hearings were about people she'd never met - two men contracted to kidnap her and then dispose of her body. Listening to the evidence had the surreal quality of watching a movie through a veil, one with the sound partially muted and a plot that seemed too improbable. It was. The plan had not come to pass, but only by a fluke series of events.

She glanced at her son, but he was intent on his sketching. Timothy seemed not to notice the defence attorney mentioning his father's name. Maybe he didn't recognize the given name, knowing him only as daddy. But the judge was undeterred by the defence trying to lay blame at her husband's feet. Her *ex*-husband, she reminded herself, or soon-to-be ex. For now, the judge was interested only in the chosen actions and intents of these two accused men.

As the testimony continued over the next days, Elizabeth learned more than she ever wanted to know. While she had thought, had hoped, that these were spur-of-the-moment actions by her husband, it was now clear that his plan had taken months in the making. How had she not read the signs, picked up on the fact that there was something seriously wrong with her marriage?

She glanced at Timothy. He gave no appearance of listening to the proceedings. He wouldn't understand, anyway. The words they were using would be foreign to such a small child. Plus, he didn't speak, so how could he understand what these strangers were saying?

"Court will recess for thirty minutes. Mrs. Whitmore, may I have a word with you in my chambers?" Although phrased as a request, Elizabeth felt like it was more of an order. She reached for Timothy's hand, but he evaded her. Instead, she wrapped her fingers gently around his upper arm and helped him off the pew. Making sure he had his Etch-a-Sketch secure in his grip, she led her son to the front of the courtroom and out the door on the left that the clerk held open for them.

As she entered his office, the judge glanced up from his

papers. "Mrs. Whitmore, I requested your presence, not that of you and your son." His eyes peered intently at her over the tops of his reading glasses.

She gripped her son's hand. "He's only four. He stays with me. We have no one else."

"Yes, that's what I was afraid of." He put down his fountain pen and folded his hands. "Do you really think that a courtroom is an appropriate place for a child to spend his days?"

"For now, yes. I need to be here, and he needs to be with me." She was done being intimidated by the men in her life.

Judge Bursey sighed. "Mrs. Whitmore, I'm on your side, believe it or not - yours and your son's. There is sensitive material being discussed during this trial, much of which is not appropriate for a child's ears. And it's only going to get harder when Mr. Whitmore is tried."

"I'm aware of that."

"What measures do you have in place to protect your son?"

Puzzled, Elizabeth's eyebrows lowered. "Protect? I thought that there was no more danger, now that these men are in custody." She added, "All of them."

The judge waited.

"At home we have a new and upgraded security system with cameras all around the exterior. The alarm system is on at all times. Both of our doors have double deadbolts. I keep Timothy with me; he does not leave my sight."

"That's what I was afraid of."

"Excuse me?" What was this man getting at?

He steepled his fingers. "You and this young lad here have been through a harrowing ordeal. And once you were safe, horrific accusations were made in the news and in this courtroom against someone you trusted." He watched how his words affected her. "Such things take a toll, both on an adult and on a child."

They both watched Timothy as he sat on the floor, twirling the knobs on his toy.

"It is not the intent of this court to further traumatize the boy. The facts that come out from here on in this trial are not things little boys should hear, especially about a parent. It is not appropriate for Timothy to continue to sit with you during these hearings."

It took several seconds for his words to penetrate Elizabeth's brain. What? How dare he? "I believe that I know what is best for my son, your Honor." Then, she added, "But thank you for your concern." There. Her mother would be proud that she'd remembered her upbringing.

"Mrs. Whitmore, I was not making a suggestion. I do not want to see that child in my courtroom after this week."

"But I have to be here."

"Yes, at least some of the time you do. You will need to arrange for your son's care away from this courtroom."

"I have arrangements and my son is fine with me. I am his guardian, his sole guardian now, and I decide what is right for him."

"Young lady, I applaud your determination and in other circumstances I might uphold your right to make decisions for your son. But on this point, I will not be moved. Make arrangements, or I will make them for you."

Elizabeth's eyes widened. Why would he take that tone with *her*? She was the victim here, she and Timothy. There was no one else for them now, it was just the two of them.

A knock sounded on the door. "Enter," the judge commanded.

A small woman with a shiny Afro came into the room. Elizabeth stood aside, assuming this was an employee bringing something to the judge. Instead, the woman smiled warmly as she approached Elizabeth with her hand out.

"Hello. I'm Anna Sanchez. I'm a social worker here at the courthouse."

Reflexively, Elizabeth shook her hand, but turned to Judge Bursey. "A social worker?" she asked him.

"In the case of minors, we often involve one of our social workers. Anna is very experienced and good with kids."

Steeling her spine, Elizabeth met his gaze head on. "Why would I need a social worker?"

"For the moment, she is an option. It would be good for her to meet Timothy and have him get to know her." His tone softened. "I know some of your personal history and that you don't have family to help you out at a time like this. Ms. Sanchez is an option. We have a playroom just down the hall from the courtroom you've been in. There is security outside, and your son will be perfectly fine playing in there with Ms. Sanchez."

"He'll also be perfectly fine with me as he has been and always will be." Enough with men trying to take over her life.

Judge Bursey removed his glasses. "As I said, it is not an option for Timothy to be in the courtroom from next week on. Either you arrange for his care with someone else, or you are free to discuss options with Ms. Sanchez." His direct gaze took in both women. "You are dismissed."

"Well, that was awkward." The two women stood uncomfortably in the hallway. "Follow me," continued Anna. "I'll show you the playroom."

"We don't really..."

Anna held up her hand to stanch Elizabeth's protest. "Please, Ms. Whitmore. Let's just have a look. Timothy can inspect the toys and we can chat for a few moments. It won't take long, I promise."

Anna moved to Timothy's side and commented on his drawing. It wasn't just a random remark about how pretty it was, but she studied what he'd drawn and used words to embellish what he had begun. Timothy didn't seem to mind when her finger tapped on a particular area on the screen. Usually, he didn't allow anyone to touch his Etch-a-Sketch.

She nodded at the security guard stationed midway between the courtroom they'd been in and the playroom. "Jeremy's a good guy," she explained. "He likes kids and keeps a trained eye out." Using a key attached to a coil around her wrist, she unlocked the door. "Sometimes custody disputes aren't pretty, and we need to keep the safety of the kids paramount."

"There's no custody dispute in our case."

"I know. I am familiar with your case and am sorry for all that you've been through. You and the little man here." She unlocked a door and ushered Elizabeth and Timothy inside.

Elizabeth nodded as she glanced around. Unlike some playrooms, this one wasn't decorated in bright, primary colors, designed to hype kids up. Instead, the muted colors calmed with comfy, kid-sized furniture, plenty of natural wood, and plush chairs, and cushions to sink into. A puppet theatre, doll house and miniature kitchen and living room took up one wall. They devoted the opposite side of the room to art activities - painting, crayons, chalk in more colors that Elizabeth had ever seen. Easels and drawing paper were plentiful. She knew that once he spied those supplies, Timothy wouldn't notice anything else in the room.

Anna followed his gaze. "Would you like to draw? Or paint?" The chalk drew Timothy - a new medium for him. Anna got him set up and, once she was sure he was comfortable, turned back to Elizabeth.

"You must think Judge Bursey was pretty high-handed with you." It was a statement rather than a question.

"Do you think?" She raised her head and looked at the ceiling. "I'm sorry. That's not like me, and I shouldn't take it out on you." She met Anna's eyes. "Yes, I think he was. And I no longer take well to men telling me what to do. My father did that all my life. I thought he did it out of love and care and that my husband would do the same." She looked at her son. "Boy, was I wrong about that."

"You trusted someone you loved. There's no shame in that, at least on your part."

"I was trusting and naive. I'm too old for naive and see where trust got us."

Glancing at her watch, Anna said, "Recess will be over in a few minutes and court will resume. Please believe me that, no matter how he phrased it, Judge Bursey is looking out for your son. The courtroom really is no place for a child, even a well-behaved little boy like Timothy. So far, much of what has been said might have gone over his head, although we can't be sure of that. But the parts that are coming truly are things that no child should have to hear."

"I know." Elizabeth studied the beige Berber carpet. "I'm worried, but I can't see a way out of having Timothy with me." She looked into Anna's eyes. "We have no one. And I can't trust him with anyone, not after what we've been through."

Anna put her hand on Elizabeth's arm. "I understand.

I've never been in your shoes, but I can see how you'd not want to let him out of your sight."

"I can't bear to not have him beside me."

"The bond you two have is important and will only get stronger now. But you can't do it all alone, not everything."

Elizabeth started to interrupt.

Anna continued. "I know, I know. You're a formidable woman, obviously, and women raise sons on their own every day, growing them into wonderful men. You will too, but those women don't do it one hundred percent on their own."

"Well, I'll have to. I'm so tired of people telling me how to raise my son. It feels like I'm getting it from all sides - the judge, you, and even a neighbor I hardly know and a police detective." She lowered her shoulders and her voice. "I don't mean to take this out on you. You're just doing your job and following your boss's orders, but from where I stand, the entire world is against me." In a smaller voice, "Still against me."

"It's okay to let someone in. You've been let down in the most horrific way, but not everyone is untrustworthy or out to get you. There will be people who come into your life who mean you no harm, who only want to help and be friends."

Elizabeth shook her head. "Right now, I can't see that happening."

"Sometimes ya gotta trust someone—if not for your own sake, then for Timothy's."

Chapter Five

"All rise." Again, they were back in court. Judge Bursey surveyed his courtroom before beginning. His frown deepened when his gaze landed on Elizabeth and the small boy beside her. She bowed her head toward her son, pretending she didn't see the look the judge gave them.

After listening to presentations from the defence and the prosecution, the judge motioned over the clerk. After conferring, the clerk strode to the front of the room and announced, "Please clear the courtroom for the rest of the morning. Only these people will remain - both attorneys, Ms. Anna Sanchez, Dr. Henry Henderson, Ms. Elizabeth Whitmore, and Timothy Whitmore. Will those people please move to the chairs at the front?"

Timothy was asleep, his head a dead weight on her thigh. How should she move him? Waking him before he was ready to be roused was never a good idea, and this was not the time nor place for a tantrum or a lengthy cry. Although small for his age, he was heavier than he looked when a deep sleep made him boneless.

The clerk stood in front of her. "Can I take him for you, ma'am?"

No, you most certainly cannot, were the first words that came to her mind. But her manners kicked in almost before they formed the initial thought "Thank you, but we're all right."

He looked skeptical and didn't move away.

The judge interrupted. "Ms. Whitmore, if the child is asleep and you think he won't fall off, leave him on the bench. You can stand at the end of the aisle and keep an eye on him."

Maybe that was as good as it was going to get right now. She really needed to come up with a plan for the rest of this trial.

Judge Bursey called for her attention. "Ms. Whitmore, we are gathered together for you and for your son. These last weeks we have watched your devotion to these hearings. We have also watched a four-year-old child sit here day in and day out when boys that age should be out playing."

He held up a hand to silence the words before they came from her mouth. "We have discussed my concerns before, but I see that you have made no move to make changes on your own or to avail yourself of our social worker services."

What could she say to that? While her mind scanned for a response, Judge Bursey continued.

"During our last conversation, I made suggestions. Compelling suggestions. Now I am no longer suggesting actions you should take but am insisting." His gaze met hers. Turning to his right, he gestured for Dr. Henry Henderson to stand. "Ms. Whitmore, I would like to present to you Dr. Henry Henderson. He is a court-appointed psychologist we often use in cases involving minors."

Dr. Henderson strode to Elizabeth's row and held out his hand. They both turned to the bench as Judge Bursey continued.

"Although no one can doubt your devotion to your son, we must question if his best interests are being met."

In the pause, all that was heard was Elizabeth's indrawn breath.

"I know that this might sound harsh to your ears, but it is the Court's duty to ensure the well-being of minor persons. A courtroom is not the ideal setting for a young boy to spend his days. Apart from this stifling atmosphere and restricted movement, the topics discussed are not meant for children's ears."

As Elizabeth opened her mouth to speak, he held up a hand and continued. "I understand your desire to be here each day and to be fully apprised of this case. But your presence does not require your son's presence."

He paused and looked down at his notes. "Furthermore, both you and your son have been through trauma. That is hard for anyone to deal with, but as an adult you are free to choose whether or not you seek help in working your way through all that happened to you.

"But that is not the case for your son. He cannot make that decision for himself and requires a guardian to assist him. Mrs. Whitmore, have you taken your son for help?"

"Yes, Your Honor. He has seen his pediatric neurologist frequently since our return home. His medications are being closely monitored, and the doctor is pleased with his progress and the decrease in his seizures."

"Good, good. I have no doubt that you see to his physical needs. But what about his psychological ones? His emotional ones? How is he coping with all that he has been through?"

Elizabeth glanced at her slumbering son. "It will take time, but he is settling in. He's safe in his home now where everything is familiar. He's playing. He's sleeping better." She didn't add that the latter was due to the medication she gave him before bed each night.

"What does he say about what happened?"

Elizabeth swallowed. "He doesn't really say much." When everyone just looked at her, she hurried on. "His language development is delayed. He's never spoken that much."

Dr. Henderson spoke up. "Would you say that he's talking more now than before the trauma, or less?"

How to answer that? Feeling cornered, she opted for the truth. "Less."

The doctor's smile was sympathetic. "Trauma can affect us in many ways."

The judge took over. "Here is what I have decided, Ms. Whitmore. Timothy will see a child psychologist for assessment. This assessment will take place over several sessions and involve some therapy. The number of sessions will be initially set at six, then be continued at the discretion of the psychologist. I expect you to comply with all appointments. The psychologist will report to this court monthly on young Timothy's progress and with his recommendations.

"Secondly, a home inspection will be carried out by our social worker, Ms. Sanchez. This will take place also across a number of visits, both planned and at unexpected times when she will drop in on you. Ms. Sanchez will report to this court in two months' time.

"And the third order is that this minor child will no longer be present in my court. You are free to make the arrangements you deem best for his care when you are in court, or you may avail yourself of Ms. Sanchez's services if you have scheduled them ahead of time. Ms. Sanchez assures me that if she cannot be present to be with Timothy in the playroom, then she will arrange for one of her staff to be available. As you can imagine, our playroom is a popular place, and you will need to reserve the times you want on the schedule."

Elizabeth's head whirled. She grabbed the back of the pew for support.

Dr. Henderson lightly clasped her other arm. "Judge Bursey, may I make a suggestion?"

The judge made a come-on motion with one hand.

"Perhaps if I knew when Timothy would be in the play-room, some of my sessions with him could take place there."

The judge looked to Elizabeth. "Would that meet with your approval?"

No! No! Nothing about this met with her approval, not one single thing. Who *were* these men to think they could make decisions about her life? How dare they! How dare he or anyone imply that she was not taking excellent care of her son? None of the injurious stuff that happened to them was her fault. And she was the one who got them out of it.

Examining her face carefully, Anna approached with papers in her hands. "I know that this must be a lot to take in. Here." She held out a sheaf of papers. "The Judge's orders are written here so you can take your time and read them when you get home." When Elizabeth didn't reach for the pages, she assured, "They are written in plain language, not legalese. Take these."

Judge Burscy explained that attached to the papers was Ms. Sanchez's contact information. She would answer any questions Elizabeth might have. "You have three days to respond to the documents. After that they are in effect.

33

Today is Friday. I expect to hear from you first thing Monday morning. We will meet in my chambers - you, me, and Ms. Sanchez, without your son. His presence will not be needed as we discuss these aspects of his care." His gavel sounded. "Dismissed."

Chapter Six

With his favorite video on repeat, Timothy was occupied. Elizabeth rested her forehead on the back of her wrist, her other hand cradling a cup of chamomile tea. Something soothing, only today its effect failed.

All her efforts went into calming her heartbeat, silencing her gasps, and putting on the facade of being in control. In front of the judge, that social worker, and psychologist was definitely not the time to lose it. Then they'd know for sure that she was unable to care for her son.

How had her life come to this?

Brooding is what her mother would call it. Brooding did no one any good. Maybe that was right. Elizabeth rose and entered the living room. Her son's eyes drooped; he was fighting sleep, trying to watch his show. She guided him to the couch, cuddling him beside her. Soon a nap captured them both.

The wet patch on her blouse was what she first noticed, then the absence of a little boy in her arms. She pulled the damp patch of drool from her skin. Where was Timothy?

The sound of her pot lid drawer opening clued her as to his whereabouts. That he was just opening the drawer now meant that he'd not been awake long. With an intensity she wished she matched, he spun the first lid and smiled.

He was happy. What was wrong with that? Why could not everyone see that Timothy had all that he needed to be content and safe?

As his mother, she knew best.

Could she fight this? Would a lawyer help her overturn the judge's ruling? She'd already talked to daddy's lawyer before the trial started. But they had only talked about safeguarding her finances and property. His team was untangling the efforts Jackson had made to get his hands on her money and the estate she'd inherited after her parents' death. The lawyer's aim was to ensure that she was protected, she and Timothy.

But wasn't this a protection issue? Maybe a different kind, but she and her son needed protection from the court. Yes, that made sense.

She scrolled through the contacts on her phone and made the call. "Good afternoon. May I speak to Norm Beattie, please?"

"I'm sorry, but he cannot come to the phone. May I take a message or make an appointment for you?"

"Thank you, but I am quite sure he will want to speak to me. Please tell him it is Elizabeth Whitmore calling, formerly Elizabeth Maddock, Mason's daughter."

She barely had time for a sip of tea before Norm's reassuring voice was on the line.

Pleasantries over, he got to the point. "Any problems accessing your finances? Any hassles with Jackson's attorney?"

"No, all that is fine, thank you. I appreciate how quickly you blocked Jackson from my accounts. I screen my calls and only accept a very few. I certainly would not speak to Jackson's lawyer; you suggested that if I do hear from him to refer him to you."

"Definitely. Sounds good. What can I do for you today?"

"I'm faxing you some documents the judge gave me this morning." She listened. "No, they don't have to do with Jackson exactly, but with Timothy and me." How to phrase this when it was so surreal? There wasn't really a short version.

She'd start at the beginning. "I've been attending the trial, learning all I can about what has happened. Timothy comes with me." Silence. She hurried to explain, "He's good, well-behaved in the courtroom. As long as he has his favorite toys, he's occupied and quiet." She didn't elaborate about her uneasiness over just how quiet he had become.

Cautiously Norm added, "Perhaps a little unorthodox, but likely not unheard of."

"Judge Bursey apparently doesn't agree. He doesn't think Timothy should be in the courtroom. He told me so last week, then today, he dismissed court early to talk to me. And a social worker and a psychologist. He had already laid out his plan to them."

"Plan?"

"It seems that he doesn't think I am looking after my son properly. His complaints are that I bring Timothy to court and that I haven't taken him to counseling."

"Can't you not take him to court? After all, there will be some pretty nasty evidence against his father discussed."

Was this yet another man who didn't get it? She inflicted the right amount of chill into her voice. "That is not the point. The judge questions if I am taking adequate care of my child. I take exception to that - great exception. I have nothing but my child's best interests at heart. He is well fed and clothed and cared for. I attend to all his medical needs, as I have always done. Timothy lost his grandparents and his father. I am all he has, and we stick together.

"Men that we trusted let us down. Other men have meant us harm. Our lives will no longer by governed by men, men such as this judge telling us how to run our lives."

"Elizabeth, I'm not sure what to say." The pause lengthened. "And I'm not trying to tell you want to do. My job as your attorney is to advise you."

"That's why I'm calling. I'd appreciate hearing from you as soon as you've looked over the documents I faxed you. I want your advice on how to fight this."

But now they had another man to see.

"Time to get ready, little man." She knew to keep her voice light and give Timothy plenty of time to stop his current activity before expecting him to be out the door. "Five more minutes, then we put away the pot lids."

She changed her blouse, putting the drool-stained one in the pile to go to the dry cleaners. Refreshing her make-up, she made sure she looked as put-together as she could. Apart from medications, she had something else to discuss with Dr. Muller this time.

His favorite wooden train in his hand, Timothy ignored the adults, safe now that the blood work part was over.

Dr. Muller studied the judge's orders that Elizabeth brought him. He looked up at her, uncertain. "What is it you'd like from me?"

How could it not be obvious? She sighed. "I'd like an affidavit from you stating that I am a good mother, that I take excellent care of Timothy."

"I can do that." He felt there was more coming.

"And I would appreciate anything you can add that will help me contest the judge's orders."

Muller glanced again at the papers in his hands. "What part of this do you want to contest?"

"All of it!" Shouldn't that be clear? "It is my decision on how Timothy spends his days and if I feel best having him in court with me, then that is where he'll be. He's fine. He does not disturb anyone. And, at home he is content. We don't need any psychologist or social worker poking their nose into our business. We need time alone to heal and put what happened behind us."

"I agree with your last statement." He shook his head. "I'm sorry, but I agree with the judge on the rest." He held up his hands as she started to protest. "Hear me out, please. Yes, it's your right as Timothy's guardian to make decisions for him. Under normal circumstances, you would do that well.

"But these are anything but normal circumstances. What you and Timothy went through is horrendous. A small child, especially one with delayed language skills, might have trouble processing all that happened. He's also had a loss of a parent. These are things that any loving parent would have difficulty helping him through; that's why we have child psychologists and other professionals to help at times like these. Trained professionals who can support a child's recovery."

He waited a beat, then continued. "Then, there's you."

Elizabeth straightened, her gaze intense. "What is that

supposed to mean?" This was a man she thought was on her side.

"Even though he was there with you, you have actually been through so much more than your son has. You could see all the possibilities. You now know the extent that you've been let down by someone you loved and trusted. So much has fallen on your shoulders."

Before she opened her mouth, he continued. "I know. You're about to say that you're fine. And you are, at least outwardly. My specialty is not psychiatry, but there is some overlap with neurology, and I have some idea of what trauma does to the brain. You've been in mamma bear mode - you've had to be. But that hypervigilance takes a toll, not just on your body but on your brain. This height-ened state of arousal leads you to make decisions that are crucial in life and death situations. That same state might not be the most beneficial in everyday life, though.

"Your instinct is to push everyone else away, believing that you are safest with just the two of you. I get that."

"It's a fact of life. It *is* just the two of us now and we need to get used to it."

Dr. Muller nodded. "In a sense, that's true. But that does not mean that other people will not come into your lives who will be helpful to you." He nodded at the papers. "I think that is what the judge is getting at."

Elizabeth's shoulders drooped in disappointment. "You're saying that you think I should comply with the orders?"

"Comply is not the word I would have chosen. But here is what I think. Yes, it is not good for Timothy to spend his days in court and to hear things not meant for a child's ears. And yes, I believe it would be good for Timothy to receive counseling." He paused. "And for you, as well."

She stood up and reached for her son's hand. Today, Elizabeth didn't care that the doctor saw her son flinch from her touch. Dr. Muller might know how to reduce Timothy's seizures, but other than that, he was not on their side. Yet one more man she should not rely on.

Chapter Seven

Elizabeth's phone rang on the drive home. Automatically, her eyes scanned the environment, making sure they were safe, before she pressed the button on her steering wheel to put her phone into hands-free mode.

"Elizabeth, it's Norm Beattie. I've looked through the documents you faxed over. They're pretty clear."

"Yes, he used plain language, mostly. In your opinion, what are my options?"

"This firm has served your family for decades. We pride ourselves on giving you the best legal advice possible."

"That's why we rely on you. What do you advise?"

"You asked for an opinion on contesting the judge's orders. Yes, it is technically possible to do so, but our chances of winning are slim to none."

"So, what do you think I should do?"

"Comply. I know that that's not what you were hoping I'd say, but it is my opinion that the best thing you can do is to submit to the home visits and with the psychologist's appointments. Hopefully, there won't be too many of them."

"Comply? But the insinuation is that I'm not a good mother!"

"That's not exactly what it says, and I don't think you should take it that way. The judge is concerned about the well-being of your son, considering all that he's been through and that *you've* been through."

"I *know* what we've been through. I was there, remember?" She reined herself in. This was not his fault, and this definitely was not how a lady acted. "Please forgive me. This is all a shock, and you can understand that I'm a little upset."

"Certainly. Understandable. Even more reason that some counseling is in order."

"Are you suggesting that I'm not handling things for us well?"

"No, not at all. You're holding up remarkably well. But that is just it - maybe *too* well. We can all use some help from time to time, and that is what the judge is suggesting.

"In fact, in custody disputes, this type of assessment and counseling is exactly what we recommend and arrange." When she didn't reply, he added, "If you'd like, I can have my secretary send over a list of therapists we've worked with in the past."

"Thank you for your time. That won't be necessary at the moment."

She drove on. Another man crossed off her list of trusted allies.

Home, with dinner on its way and Timothy engrossed with his blocks, Elizabeth pulled a lined pad towards her.

Plan A

Part 1) Comply with the judge's ruling. Take him to see

the psychologist, Henderson, whom the judge recommended, for as many appointments as Henderson deemed
advisable. Hmm. Seemed like a money-maker for him.

Part 2) Comply with the social worker's planned and
surprised home inspection visits. That one really irked.

Part 3) Comply with not bringing Timothy to court.
That would require trusting him to the care of Anna
Sanchez in the court building's playroom. She thought a
minute, searching all possibilities. Or asking her neighbor,
Cynthia to babysit Timothy. Neither of those options sat
well with Elizabeth. How could she trust virtual strangers to
look after her son?

Plan B

Part 1) Run. This one had a certain appeal. Take
Timothy and flee the area, the country. Empty her bank
accounts. If she could get access to all that she'd inherited,
they would be set for life in some countries. Visions of the
two of them strolling along a white sand beach filled her
mind.

Part 2) This would require research - research into the
countries where they might happily settle. She'd need to
pick a safe country. One with good educational access. One
with good medical care readily available. Although she'd
travelled extensively with her parents, none of the touristy
places she'd visited appealed as a place for permanent
residency.

Part 3) Timothy's health was paramount. Anyplace
they'd go would need to be able to follow his treatment regi-
men. It would need to be a place that would freely communicate with Dr. Muller to ensure continuity with his
medication and follow-ups.

Part 4) Fleeing would mean giving up her homeland for
foreign shores. She loved her country, or used to, before its

officials intruded into her personal life. If they fled after disobeying a court mandate, there would be no coming back from this. She would give up her rights to live peacefully in her homeland. Her instinct was to get back to what had been familiar to them before the abduction. What would a whole new environment do to the peace that she was working so hard to find?

Should I stay, or should I go? That old song flashed into her mind. Jackson used to sing it. This was way back, early in their marriage, when his playful side came out often, that side she fell in love with. Everything in her home growing up was formal; Jackson was like a fresh spring breeze blowing into her life. His fun and spontaneity appealed to her, even if less so to her parents. She hummed the '80s song under her breath. It surprised her that a smile formed on her lips. Maybe her life with Jackson had not been all bad. Of course not - Timothy came out of that union.

A pot lid fell to the floor. Its momentum could not last forever. Maybe nothing did.

Dinner, cleaning up the kitchen, bathing Timothy, reading to him, and tucking him into bed. The little things, the routines that filled up the minutes of their day, fulfilling them and bringing them closer.

Elizabeth reviewed her list again.

What would daddy do?

Running was not his style. No, he'd turn and fight, standing up for his family, for what was right.

Her lawyer felt that complying was what was right. Could that be true? She needed to look at this objectively.

Hah! How could she be objective about her life?

Her mother was the quiet one in their family, but when it mattered, her opinions held weight. Appearances were important to her, and she would look at things from an outsider's point of view. How would an impartial stranger regard this situation?

Wait. Wasn't that supposed to be a judge's role - an impartial stranger, weighing the evidence from both sides?

Ah, but he was only human and fallible. He didn't know Elizabeth, not really, and he certainly didn't know Timothy. It was possible that he had jumped to the wrong conclusions.

Yet, Norm Beattie didn't think they should contest the ruling, that it would not go the way she wanted. On the plus side though, it would delay things. Was that an advantage? Would putting off the inevitable make it easier for her to handle? Or would it be better to just get it over with so that their lives could return to normal?

Elizabeth had always been the good girl. After what their family had been through when she was a child, she felt the unspoken burden to never cause her parents additional grief. Plus, it wasn't in her nature to create disturbances. So why did complying feel so wrong?

Sleeping on it helped. Elizabeth woke with new resolve. While slumbering, her subconscious worked out why she was so opposed to complying with the judge.

All her life she'd acquiesced, giving in, and following the lead of others. Her brother still died. Her parents still died. Her husband tried to have her killed, and a stranger had tried to kill her son. Yeah, like being obedient had really worked for her.

Attempting to look at things impartially, she realized that not complying could suggest that she had something to hide. There was a difference between being a private person and hiding deep, dark secrets.

There was nothing to hide. Thanks to Jackson and Russell Rose Allen, the entire world knew about her life, or at least that's how it felt. For a private person, this was painful. Her private life would be shredded even more once the social worker and psychologist started prying their way inside her locked doors.

After Timothy fell asleep, Elizabeth had stayed up late researching grief and therapy. Following the strands of beliefs about post-traumatic stress disorder was like leaping headfirst down a rabbit hole.

The common thought seemed to be that simply putting something traumatic behind you didn't work. There could be long-term repercussions; she didn't want that for Timothy.

What if she had had therapy at age nine when her brother died? Would she feel the weight of guilt any less now? Had that one swimming incident shaped her life forever?

She thought of the quiet household where she grew up. Never a boisterous place, it became somber when it was just the three of them left, as if that one light, their hub extinguished with her brother's death. It had felt wrong to laugh out loud, disrespectful to his memory. Is that what she wanted for Timothy - to never feel free to laugh, a full-throttle belly laugh?

It hurt to think anything negative about her parents. They had loved her; of that she was sure. They took excellent care of her, treating her as something fragile to be handled delicately.

This evidence of their care had seemed normal, and it was soothing being cherished. But had it equipped her for life? Daddy had thought he'd be around for a long time, but who knew? There were no guarantees. Her upbringing of always being taken care of, of having a man make the decisions and watch out for her had created a mindset that had worked against her during the abduction. Maybe if she'd thought more for herself, she'd have recognized the signs that something was seriously wrong with her marriage. Maybe if she'd relied on herself, she would have gotten herself and Timothy out of Russel Rose's hands far earlier and spared them some additional trauma.

She was still a young woman. She could change. She had changed. She'd done what she had to do to save her son. Now, she would do so again.

With a clearer head, she planned her strategy. Yes, she would comply, but on her terms. This felt better, not so much like caving in.

To start with, she'd prefer not to use the court-appointed psychologist. Dr. Henry Henderson had seemed an all-right fellow, but he was not *her* choice. While the judge had picked him, Elizabeth had not. She was through with men deciding for her. The judge's documents clearly stated a psychologist and a social worker as the people to interfere in her life. While the social work portion specifically mentioned Anna Sanchez, the psychologist was unnamed.

Who better to understand her point of view - a mother's point of view, than a woman? Surely there were excellent female psychologists around.

She started with the State College of Psychologists. That was overwhelming. A degree in interior design hadn't equipped her to know much about psychology.

Next, she looked up what it took to become a psychologist. Ah, some had credentials at the master's degree level, and some had doctorates. Well, the more training the better if they were going to work with Timothy.

Returning to the College of Psychologists, she was

better able to narrow her search to only those with PhDs. She learned that not every psychologist was licensed to work in every aspect of psychology. They needed to gain competencies in their areas. She narrowed things further to those who worked with children.

Clicking on a psychologist's name generally brought up their picture. Not always, though. There was something off about a counselor who did not want you to see their face or was too insecure about their self-image to post their photo. Or maybe they just couldn't be bothered. Her mother used to stress that it's attention to the minor details that mattered. Elizabeth refined her list of possible psychologists further by location; she did not want to spend hours driving to appointments. And by sex, of course. She wanted to work with a woman.

She considered them candidates. Only the best were fit to work with her son. Each candidate listed their qualifications in a curriculum vitae, their areas of competencies and interests. Some were not taking new clients, but most were.

Elizabeth honed her list to her top four choices. Next, she turned to internet searches to learn more about these women.

The name that turned up the most hits was that of Dr. Hanna Mayberry. A nice name, a pleasant one - the sort you could trust. Elizabeth smiled to herself. She had no idea where that thought came from, just that she liked the sound of the name.

Dr. Mayberry did not specialize in children, although she saw children. Her caseload was eclectic for age and sex. And for presenting difficulties. Maybe she was a woman who liked a challenge, or maybe she just got bored easily and liked diversity. That suited Elizabeth just fine; such a psychologist might be willing to stick to just the initial six visits, then happily dismiss them.

The search pulled up award after award that Dr. Mayberry had won. She didn't appear to seek this attention but her pro bono work and her willingness to take on cases no one else would have had people lauding her praises. She took on tough cases; well, what would be more difficult than doing talk therapy with a four-year-old who didn't talk?

Dr. Mayberry did not restrict herself to any specific area of psychology. She accepted referrals from forensic psychiatrists. She did Fitness to Stand Trial assessments. Workmen's Compensation retained her services, especially for return to work or retraining assessments. Occasionally, she worked with those rare clients diagnosed with dissociated personality disorder. She did court work in child custody and access disputes. The common thread throughout her caseload was trauma. Yes, she seemed like the best choice of all the psychologists Elizabeth researched.

Chapter Eight

Sunday rushed by. Grateful for Timothy's ability to amuse himself for long stretches of time without demanding her attention, Elizabeth focused on her petition to the court and went to bed satisfied that she had presented her case well.

Yes, she would comply with Judge Bursey's ruling, but with a few amendments of her own. She requested the right to cancel or refuse a visit from the social worker if Timothy was ill. And he was ill often due to his seizure disorder. While each seizure lasted less than two minutes, but could seem like hours at the time, they left him disoriented and exhausted. He often slept for the rest of the day. Surely the court would understand. This would give Elizabeth some control over the visits.

She would agree to keep her son out of the courtroom except for circumstances where she could not find appropriate childcare. Again, anyone with a heart would understand that.

Third, she would take Timothy to see a psychologist, but one of her choosing. Her brief explained the extensive research she had carried out, her reasons for choosing Dr. Mayberry and included a few citations listing the psychologist's accolades.

She sent her packet to the courthouse by courier and phoned for an appointment with Judge Bursey. A clerk told her to come in at 2:45.

"Ms. Whitmore, you've been busy." He looked pointedly at Timothy's feet dangling off of the sofa, absorbed in his Thomas the Tank engine toy. "But what is that child doing here?"

"Court is not in session today, so he is with me. You said that you did not want to see him in court, and I will do my best to make sure that does not happen." She nodded at her petition centered on his desk. "But, as I explained there, although I will do my best to find childcare for him, there could be the odd occasion when I will have no choice but to have him with me. We have no family, as you are aware."

"I get that. My daughter has sporadic childcare emergencies; she's lucky that my wife can step in to help her." He shuffled the pages. "I appreciate how difficult this is for you, and that I have forced you to do something you find uncomfortable. I assure you I am doing this for the sake of the child."

"I think I understand your motivations, Your Honor."

"Now, about the psychologist. I am familiar with the work of Dr. Mayberry. She has testified in this court on several occasions. Her work is well-respected. I would have preferred that you and Timothy work with Dr. Henderson; I specifically chose him for your situation. But I will grant your petition. How soon will your son begin seeing her?"

"I'm not sure. I haven't contacted her yet; I wanted to

make sure that you were in agreement before making a commitment."

His smile said that it saw through her. "Very well. By the end of this week submit to the clerk a schedule for your initial six appointments." He slipped her papers into a file folder. "But, if Dr. Mayberry is unavailable, make those appointments with Dr. Henderson. You do realize that someone with a reputation like Dr. Mayberry may well not be able to fit you in on short notice?"

"Good day. You have reached the office of Dr. Mayberry. This is Doris speaking. How may I help you?"

"My name is Elizabeth Whitmore. I would like to make an appointment for my son, Timothy."

"I'm sorry, but Dr. Mayberry isn't taking new clients."

No! This is *not* how this was going down.

"It is crucial that I speak with Dr. Mayberry." No begging or pleading. Just calm assertion.

Doris laughed. "I'm sorry, but do you know how many times people have said that? It is just not possible for Dr. Mayberry to work with all the people who would like to see her. There just are not enough hours in the day."

"This is different."

Doris gave a sniff.

"If I could have just a few minutes of her time, I am sure that she would agree to see my son."

Something twigged Doris's memory. "What did you say your name is again?"

"Elizabeth Whitmore and my son is Timothy Whitmore."

"Are you the one….?"

"Yes. Were you about to ask, 'Are you the ones who have been in a media circus, the ones kidnapped and almost killed'?"

"I didn't mean to be insensitive. That came out wrong. Would you hold on a minute, please?" Without waiting for an answer, she was gone and in her place a sitar played, layered on the sounds of a waterfall.

"Dr. Mayberry says that she has a cancellation later this afternoon. If you could come in at 4:45, she can spare fifteen minutes to talk with you." She hastened to add, "No guarantees. This is just an initial meeting. She really is booked quite full."

"We'll be there." She hung up as Doris was telling her to wait, Dr. Mayberry meant just Elizabeth.

Next, another difficult phone call.

"Ms. Sanchez? This is Elizabeth Whitmore from court. You gave me your number to arrange for my son to spend time in the playroom while I attend court. Would it be possible for ninety minutes tomorrow morning?"

"Definitely. I had already blocked the time into my schedule and was expecting your call. Would you like to come say fifteen minutes early to help Timothy get used to the room and me before you have to leave?" She added, "Not that I expect there to be any problems; he seemed comfortable the last time, but I'd like *you* to be comfortable as well."

"Thank you for your consideration and we'll do that." Comfortable? No, there was not one thing about this that felt comfortable for Elizabeth.

"Good day, Ms. Whitmore. Please, have a seat. And who is this?"

"This is my son, Timothy." Turning to the child, "Timothy, could you say hello to Dr. Mayberry?"

No response.

Dr. Mayberry got to her knees in front of Timothy. With her best non-threatening smile, she welcomed him to her office. "Hi there, little man." His eyes momentarily met hers, and then slid off. "It's nice to see you, Tim."

"Timothy. His name is Timothy, not Tim."

"I'll remember that." No kidding, I will, thought Dr. Mayberry. "Would you like Timothy to wait in the other room while we talk? Doris, my receptionist, will keep an eye on him. She's good with kids."

Elizabeth rested a hand on Timothy's shoulder. "No. No, thank you. Timothy stays with me."

"You might feel that you can speak more freely if he is not within hearing distance."

"He's fine. He doesn't pay attention to things around him, anyway."

Interesting, thought Dr. Mayberry.

Elizabeth settled Timothy at the coffee table, pulling a coloring book and crayons from her shoulder purse.

"We'll be careful what we say, anyway." Dr. Mayberry smoothed her hands down the back of her skirt before sitting down in the chair across from the couch. "What brings you to my office today?"

"I hoped that you would agree to see Timothy, to see us." She pulled from her over-sized handbag a copy of the judge's orders and handed them over. "As you can see, Judge Bursey feels that Timothy needs to see someone and be evaluated after the experiences we had." She glanced around the office while Dr. Mayberry perused the pages, appreciating the calming, muted colors.

"That doesn't seem to be all that concerned him."

"No. He didn't like that I brought Timothy with me to court. He doesn't understand that Timothy ignores most of what goes on around him."

"How do you know that he ignores things?"

"Well, look at him." She gestured beside her knees to where her son carefully drew. "He gets so engrossed in whatever he's doing." Proudly, she added, "His concentration is impressive for someone of his age."

"How old is he?"

"Four, almost five."

"I haven't heard him say much. Does he talk to you about how he's feeling?"

Elizabeth shook her head. "He rarely speaks. He makes noises and I can interpret most of them, guessing what he wants."

Dr. Mayberry waited.

Elizabeth filled the silence. "He used to talk more - some phrases and basic things. He has a language delay. Dr. Muller, his pediatric neurologist, says that it's likely related to his seizure disorder and that speech will come in time."

"Has he seen a speech/language pathologist?"

Elizabeth shook her head. "We talked about a referral, but haven't yet. With everything that's happened to us, we're still trying to catch our breath."

Nodding her understanding, Dr. Mayberry changed the subject. "Can you tell me in your own words what it is you would like from me?" She laid the court papers on the coffee table, near to Timothy's elbow. It would be interesting. She carefully did not directly eye either the tempting papers, or the child.

"What I want is a report for the court saying that I take good care of Timothy, and that his needs are being met. His neurologist is writing a letter about my son's physical care. I would appreciate something from you about his psychological well-being." She reached for the court papers. "The judge stipulates a minimum of six visits with a psychologist, with additional appointments at the discretion of the psychologist. But I think that six will be fine. You'll see that Timothy is a well-behaved child. Tantrums are very rare with him. As long as I give him warning about a change of activities, he's pretty compliant."

"Is that a good thing?"

Elizabeth's head tilted to one side. "Do you have children, Dr. Mayberry?"

"No."

"Then you might not be able to appreciate having an obedient child. It makes life so much easier and more pleasant for both of us."

Dr. Mayberry gave a neutral but encouraging expression, one practiced and perfected over many years. "You realize that if I agree to work with you, I am bound by both my professional ethics and by this court order to cite my honest appraisal of what is going on with your son. Are you willing to abide by this?"

"Of course. I researched you and several other psychologists. You were my top pick, based on your experience and reputation. I trust that you will find that Timothy is just fine."

"The word 'fine' can be construed in many ways, but we'll get into that if I agree to take you and your son on as clients." Then, she added, "Please understand that I mean that - you and your son. This will require both separate sessions with each of you individually and sometimes together."

"Individual? Can't you just see us together? After all,

you are supposed to be judging my interactions with my son."

"If I become involved, I will look at various aspects of both your son's care and his development. Are you comfortable with that?"

Elizabeth tried to shake off that feeling of being boxed in. She hated that helpless feeling and had vowed never to allow herself to be in such a situation again. This time, though, she reminded herself that she had taken control. *She* had chosen this psychologist and convince the judge to let go of his hand-picked psychologist in favor of the one that Elizabeth preferred. How the psychologist conducted her evaluation was a professional decision. She'd need to trust this woman.

Dr. Henry Murphy picked up the call just before it went to voicemail. "Hello."

"Murph! I caught a good one today."

"Nice to hear the enthusiasm in your voice." It had been a while since his friend and protégé Hanna Mayberry had gushed about anything.

"Yeah, it's been a while. But I have a feeling in my bones that this one's going to light my fire."

"Tell me about it."

"You heard in the news about that woman and her kid who were snatched by that escaped patient? Then her husband was trying to have her whacked at the same time."

"Interesting. Lots to untangle there."

"Well, she has the proverbial stick up her you-know-what, but the kid is the one who turned my crank. There's something different there."

"You don't usually go for kids."

"Never say never. Maybe it's my biological clock ticking that made this kid appealing to me. But there's a lot more going on there than even the mother seems to realize."

"How so?"

"He didn't say a word, and I take it that that's not unusual, especially since the kidnapping."

"You're thinking it's selective mutism?"

"Maybe, but I wouldn't jump to that. There were language delays pre-trauma. And he doesn't seem that anxious.

"The mom was fine talking in front of him because she said he pays no attention to anything but what he is doing. He focused intently and there was no eye contact to show his interest in us."

"What did he do?"

"He colored. She brought this coloring book, just a typical little kid's kind, and crayons. The boy didn't color in or out of the lines. Instead, he embellished the line drawings, enhancing and improving them. Pretty impressive dexterity for a four-year-old."

"What do they want from you? Does she expect you to get her child talking again?"

"This is a court-ordered assessment and treatment block. I had the sense that if a judge had not ordered this, that her son would be seeing no one. She's pretty closed off."

Chapter Nine

Asking others for help didn't sit well with Elizabeth. She battled trust issues. She was a private person, raised that way. She hated that so much of her private business and pain was public knowledge, but it was worse since she couldn't cocoon at home with Timothy and lick her wounds away from prying eyes.

In her family, they relied on each other. When they needed outside help, they paid for it, such as with lawyers and accountants.

Now Elizabeth needed help and needed to ask for that help from people who were close to being strangers. Timothy sat on the grass behind her, spinning a frisbee in the palm of one hand.

Cynthia must have seen her coming across the lawn because she opened the door almost as soon as Elizabeth knocked.

"How lovely to see you! How are you?" She opened the door wider and stuck her head out. Spying Timothy, she yelled over her shoulder, "Amy! Timothy's here."

"We're just here for a minute. I didn't mean to disturb you."

"Nonsense, come in, come in." A whirling flash of fluffy dog and little girl raced by, landing in a heap beside Timothy. His frisbee went flying, Blitz scurrying after it.

Elizabeth cringed at the thought of dog slobber all over her son's toy and she debated the best ways of sanitizing it later.

"Come on, let's go swing." Amy grabbed Timothy's hand and pulled him after her into the back yard.

Worried, Elizabeth watched to make sure that her son wasn't upset at the loss of his toy, that this girl had touched him, or that he was moving out of sight of his mother. Maybe he was in shock.

"Rather than coming in, would you mind if we followed the children? I'd like to keep my eye on Timothy."

"Sure. I'll grab some iced tea and meet you out back. Make yourself at home."

Amy had left the gate open, so Elizabeth carefully latched it behind her. Out back she found the two children on a teeter totter. This was something new for Timothy; he was hanging on for dear life, but Amy was pushing them gently. Timothy's scrunched-up face relaxed slightly, and a grin overtook his grimace. Blitz, or whatever his name was, lay in the grass near their feet, chewing on her son's frisbee. Well, he could have it; she was buying Timothy a new one, one without dog slobber.

Cynthia's hip pushed open the back door. She deposited a tray on the rattan table, then said she'd be right back. She hurried around the side of the house and was back within half a minute. "Just had to check that we shut the gate. Sometimes Amy forgets, especially when she has a friend over. I'd hate for Blitz to get out."

That was her worry, questioned Elizabeth? Maybe she should rethink what she was about to ask. Could this woman truly look after her son? What were her options? She had the next two mornings lined up for Timothy at the court's playroom, but nothing arranged for Thursday and Friday morning. She didn't have time to check out day care centers; the thought of dropping her son off with strangers who were looking after dozens of small children en masse churned her stomach. How easy would it be to lose one small boy, especially a quiet one, in that herd of children? No, for now, there was no choice but to throw herself on the mercy of this woman, this neighbor.

Cynthia poured two glasses of tea as she and Elizabeth settled themselves in matching chairs. "I'm glad you brought Timothy over. Amy's restless and looking for something to do. Timothy is just what she needed."

The kids were getting along well. Amy seemed not to mind or not to notice that their conversation was all one-sided. Timothy followed her lead and appeared happy to do so.

Cynthia watched the children but observed Elizabeth out of the corner of her eye. She asked, "I hope it's okay, but I'm in the habit of speaking my mind." She waited, but Elizabeth just sipped her tea. "You seem uncomfortable. Is there something bothering you?" She hastened to add, "If you don't want to talk, that's okay. We can just sit here, soak up the sun and enjoy the kids."

Soak up the sun? Didn't she know that that was bad for you? Elizabeth had not thought to put sunscreen on herself or on Timothy. She took a deep breath. The sooner she got this over with, the sooner they'd be out of here. "I need to ask you a favor."

"Sure, anything."

Elizabeth gave a half-smile. "Don't be too quick to agree. You don't know what it is yet."

"I've an idea. You want me to watch Timothy for you. Sure."

Elizabeth blinked. It was that easy? "But you don't know when?"

Cynthia laughed. "This," she indicated the yard with her hand, "is pretty much how we spend our days lately, or a mix between playing out here and inside. You may have noticed that we don't go out much."

No, Elizabeth hadn't noticed. But she noticed that there seemed to be just Cynthia and Amy around. Hadn't there been a man some years back?

"I'm sorry, but I really know little about you or any of the other neighbors." How to phrase this delicately? "Is there just you and Amy here?" Hopefully, that was polite enough for a nosy question.

"Yes, it's just the two of us since Hugh passed away." She tilted her head at Elizabeth. "I'm not sure you ever met him, but Jackson did. Hugh died almost two years ago. Cancer. It was fast."

Elizabeth's hand went to her throat. How insensitive could she be? Here she was wallowing in her own problems when this woman had endured so much. "I'm so sorry. Please accept my deepest condolences. I didn't know." She placed her glass on the tray. "Timothy and I will get out of your hair. We didn't mean to disturb you."

"Don't be silly! Sit back down. Here." She refilled Elizabeth's glass. "I'll admit that it was tough that first half year. It was like a part of us had died with him. But this spring we both started to come back to life. It's not good for a little one to remain in a house of mourning. This is our life now, without him, and we have to get used to it. I still need to be a mother and Amy needs to be a little girl."

Elizabeth swallowed, her eyes battling tears. She would not let this brave woman see her cry.

"When do you need me to babysit Timothy?"

And it was that easy.

Not that Elizabeth felt good about leaving Timothy with anyone, but maybe with this woman, she could bear it.

Now if she could only bear to hear discussed in court exactly what her soon-to-be-ex-husband had planned for her.

Chapter Ten

"You'll take turns today," explained Dr. Mayberry. "We'll begin with the two of you in here, then just you alone, then I'll spend some time with Timothy."

"I'm not sure that will work. I'm more comfortable if you meet with both of us together."

"In our initial meeting, before I agreed to take you on as clients, I explained the structure that we'll follow."

"Yes. Yes, you did, but I hoped that once you got to know us, you'd see us as a team - sort of package deal."

"You are a package; you're a family. But families are made up of individual members." She picked up her pen and clipboard. "Some things will be just about you; some will be just about your son. And some will be about the two of you interacting together."

That brought Elizabeth back to images from her youth. Most of her growing-up years, it had been the three of them. Were they individuals, melding into a team, or had she been an add-on to her parent's partnership? Or were she and her mother hangers-on to her father's leadership?

Were these the sort of things they'd discuss in Dr. Mayberry's sessions?

This time Timothy focussed on his Etch-a-Sketch, although Elizabeth's bag held an assortment of toys designed to keep him quiet.

Dr. Mayberry noticed. "He *can* concentrate intently for one so young."

Any mother would be proud of that. "Yes, he can. He focuses and plays quietly for long stretches of time."

"Is that a good thing?"

"Why, yes, of course. I hear mothers complaining that they can't get anything done because their child is at them all the time. Timothy is self-contained and not the needy type."

"Hmmm."

"Being able to amuse and motivate yourself is a blessing to me and a skill he'll put to good use later in life."

"Why do you think it is that many mothers feel overwhelmed by the amount of time their toddler or preschooler demands of them?"

"Perhaps they have not trained their child to be independent. Or set down rules and routines."

"What did you do to teach Timothy to play for such long periods on his own?"

That gave Elizabeth pause. "I don't really know. Maybe it was just the expectations we had for him. I'm not sure that we really insisted; he might have just done this on his own."

"Do you think that children come the way they are, with their unique personalities, or that we, as parents, shape the people our children are?"

"That's a little heavy for two o'clock in the afternoon,

isn't it?" Elizabeth quipped to hide her discomfort. How to answer such a question?

"Never mind. Some of what I'll throw out doesn't demand an answer. Sometimes these are just thinking points."

Timothy made a noise, something between a groan and a whine. It was the sound he made when frustrated when a tantrum might be building. Elizabeth rose and went to him. He rocked back and forth.

"Oh," she said. "The knob on the Etch-a-Sketch is stuck again. We really should get a new one."

"Or teach him how to handle it when things don't go as expected."

Elizabeth looked up quickly. "Oh, we've had more experience than we needed recently about things not going as expected." She worked the knob until it turned freely again. Timothy's rocking slowed down as she returned the toy to him.

"Do you want to talk about the experiences that brought you here?"

Elizabeth nodded. "As you read in the court documents, this was Judge Bursey's idea."

This was not quite what Dr. Mayberry meant by recent 'experiences', but she let Elizabeth run with it. For now.

"He took exception to Timothy being in the courtroom. He doesn't know Timothy, so doesn't realize that my son does not pay attention to what is going on around him." She reflected a moment. "That was maybe a blessing when we were being held by that man."

"That man?"

"Russell Rose Allen, the guy who took us."

Steadily watching Timothy, Dr. Mayberry thought she detected a shift in his posture. "Go on," she encouraged.

"Timothy didn't bother anyone and didn't disturb the court proceedings in any way."

"Did they disturb him?"

Elizabeth shook her head. "I've already explained that my son is oblivious to anything he's not directly involved in."

"And while he's engrossed in his toys, do you think he's listening to what's going on around him?"

"Not really." Elizabeth watched her son. "You may have noticed that he doesn't speak much. Well, lately, hardly at all. He has a language delay."

"Have you had that assessed?"

"Not yet. It's on the list of things to do. The priority has been to get his seizures under control. They were heading the right way until he had to be without his medications while we were, ah, away. But things are getting back on track now. The seizures have lessened in both frequency and intensity. Dr. Muller, his pediatric neurologist, is pleased with how things are going."

"What does he say about Timothy's language development?"

"Some of the seizure activity is in the left side, in Broca's area, so that may have caused the language delay."

"When did the seizures start?"

"Around his second birthday."

"How was his expressive language up to then?"

"He used a few words. He also made sounds and we pretty much knew what he was asking for."

"How does he communicate now?"

"Communicate?"

"You know, make his wants and needs known?"

Elizabeth frowned. "He's four. He doesn't have a lot of

wants and needs. He has everything he wants - it's all provided for him."

"How does he show his preference when you give him several choices?"

"I'm not really sure. That situation doesn't come up often. When it does, I can guess what he wants."

Dr. Mayberry let that one go. For now. "So, all this," she gestured around her office, "has come about because the Judge didn't appreciate your son's presence in court?"

"Pretty much, yes, I'd say that's it. He anticipated that more sensitive and personal testimony would be coming in future sessions and didn't feel that those were things that Timothy should hear. Again, he doesn't understand about Timothy."

"You do?"

Was that a question or a statement? "Yes."

"Let's look at that a moment more. You say that your son doesn't listen to things, conversations going on around him. Is he listening to us now?"

Elizabeth glanced at her son and shook her head. "No, I'm pretty sure not."

"Have you had his hearing checked?"

"Yes; when he had his two-year-old vaccinations, the nurse expressed concern about him not talking and referred us to an audiologist. The audiologist said that assessments were not conclusive with one so young, but her tests would give us an idea. He seemed to react to the tones through the headphones, so she felt that bilaterally his hearing was within normal limits."

"May I caution you about something?" She didn't wait for Elizabeth's response. "Have you heard that old saying, 'Little pitchers have big ears'? Well, some of these sayings are still in existence because they have validity.

"Children can appear totally immersed in what they are doing, while taking in all that the adults around them are saying." She held up her hand to halt whatever Elizabeth was about to say. "Even children who do not *use* language may have the ability to *understand* language. He may take in far more than you suspect."

They both stared at Timothy. His body language did not alter.

"I would suggest you keep this in mind and be aware of what is said in his presence. This is true for any child, but especially concerning when a child may not have the language skills to process and discuss what he is hearing."

Elizabeth's eyes widened. She looked from her son to Dr. Mayberry and back again. Her mind went back over conversations she'd had, things he might have overheard. Thankfully, there weren't many since they spent most of their time alone. Although, those first few days home, the television news had been on almost incessantly as she tried to make herself aware of all that was being said about them and the extent of the betrayal they'd suffered.

"Now, may I ask if you'd please wait in the other room? I'd like a bit of time alone with your son." At Elizabeth's hesitation, she added, "He needs to get to know me. I'll just break the ice this time. Remember that part of the court order is my assessment. I'll need to spend time with Timothy. Alone."

Elizabeth gathered her purse and rose. Kneeling by Timothy, she said, "All right, little man. You heard Dr. Mayberry." At least, she wondered if he had. "I'll be right outside this door and I'll see you in a few minutes." She noticed the psychologist laying out paper and crayons. "Look. See what Dr. Mayberry has?" She took his chin in her hands to point his face in the direction of the coffee table. "Will you go with me to the table?"

Obediently, Timothy took her outstretched hand and knelt by the side of the coffee table. Elizabeth put the Etch-a-Sketch in her bag and rose. "Mommy will be back for you in just a few minutes." She watched, but he showed no reaction to her retreat. She entered the waiting room but left the door to the office ajar. Timothy might not have separation anxiety, but *she* did.

"Hello little man," Dr. Mayberry said, using his mother's words. "Will you come draw with me?" Dr. Mayberry picked up a crayon and drew the rough outline of a car. Her approximation wasn't good, but in her experience, kids guessed what she was trying to make. In this case, her lines were even more ambiguous. She wanted to see if Timothy responded to her words.

She moved the paper in front of Timothy. "I'm not very good at this. Can you help me with this car?" She placed a fresh package of eight differently colored crayons centered just past the top of the paper. Timothy reached, then hesitated. After a few softly spoken, encouraging words, he chose a black crayon and completed the wheels on the car.

Yes! Either he had stupendous visual processing skills and could figure out what her few pencil strokes meant to convey, or he had heard and understood when she said that this was supposed to be a car. He confirmed her hunch when he added windows and headlights. She turned her head away and smiled the kind of smile she never let her clients see.

Chapter Eleven

As if this hadn't been a rough enough week, why couldn't people leave her alone? The doorbell rang for the third time. Checking the camera, she saw that there were three images on the screen, a man with his back to the camera, surveying the street, a woman, and a child. Surely a reporter wouldn't bring his family.

The man turned and smiled at something the woman said. Jake - the cop who'd been there when everything went down at that sleazy hotel. He said he'd be back. And, as he'd threatened, this time he had his girlfriend and her son in tow. What would make him think that she wanted to meet new people?

He was persistent. He had to know that she wouldn't appreciate this, but he kept pushing the doorbell, anyway. She sighed. He obviously wasn't going away. She owed the guy some measure of courtesy for his part in their rescue, but that gratitude only went so far. She didn't need him or his friends in her life now.

Timothy went to the door, drawn by the repeated peal

of the bell. She'd had the deadbolts installed up, out of his reach, but he tried anyway. One day he would be tall enough, but she had time to teach him about danger long before he could work the knobs on his own.

But Jake was no threat. Not physically, anyway, although he was a threat to her peace of mind. Why could he not leave her alone?

Elizabeth undid the locks. With one hand holding Timothy firmly behind her, she opened the door. "Good evening, Jake. What brings you here on a Friday evening?"

Jake looked pointedly at the locked screen door.

Elizabeth pushed the lever to unlatch it.

Jake opened the door, ushering the woman and child inside. Timothy peered around his mother's leg. Daniel did the same with his mother. The boys eyed each other. The adults waited. Daniel took one step forward, then hesitated.

"Daniel," his mother reminded him, "do you want to show Timothy your blocks?"

That was the starter he needed. Daniel plopped to the floor and unzipped his backpack. Digging in, he pulled out a brightly colored Thomas the Tank engine block.

Timothy let go of his mom's pant leg and ran into the living room. He returned almost immediately with a similar block in his hand. Holding it out to Daniel, he retreated to the other room, Daniel and his backpack following.

"Do you think we should have introduced them?" Keira asked. Then she held out her hand to Elizabeth. "Hi. Since this lug doesn't seem to recall that we've never met, I'll do the honors." The women shook. "Hi. I'm Keira Foster." She pointed to the other room. "And that is my son, Daniel."

"Pleased to meet you." Elizabeth said the right words, but she glared at Jake. "I'm Elizabeth Whitmore, and that was my son, Timothy." She waited for Jake to explain their presence.

Keira took over instead. "Yes, I know who you are." She laughed. "It must seem to you that the entire world knows about you."

Elizabeth flinched.

"That's tough," Keira continued. "I know that I'd hate it. That's why I thought that you could use a friend. Well, Jake and I thought that."

Jake nudged her.

"Yeah, it was his idea first, but I agreed. Plus, Timothy could probably use someone safe to play with."

"Well, he has me."

"Tell me about it! Yeah, I know what it's like to be a single mom, having to be all things to your kid on your own. I can do it, mind you, and have done it for years." She bumped Jake's hip with her own. "I needed some persuasion to see that it's easier when you let someone else help, even just a bit." She eyed Elizabeth. "I'd guess that you're in the same position."

Since they were here anyway, and the boys seemed to have taken to each other, Elizabeth invited the couple into the living room. It was strange. They watched the two boys who seemed in synch with each other, although neither had said a word, as far as the adults could tell. They sometimes followed each other's actions, but mostly played alongside each other, building, and creating structures meaningful only to them.

Feeling that Timothy would be safe with these people, Elizabeth excused herself to make coffee. It looked like the trio had invited themselves to stay for a while.

Coffee in hand, Keira stated the obvious, "You don't want us here."

Elizabeth's ingrained courtesy took over. "It's not you per se. I have nothing against you or your son." She pointedly did not look at Jake.

Jake grinned and rested his arm along the back of the couch.

"I think I'm still in shock; we're still in shock and trying to recover." Elizabeth continued. "I have trust issues."

"Hah!" Jake chuckled.

Keira elbowed him. "Tell me about it," she said.

Elizabeth tilted her head and regarded Keira.

"Jake can tell you about my trust issues. I'm probably the least trusting person he's met."

"And yet…" Elizabeth nodded between the two of them.

"Oh, she made me work for it." Jake dodged Keira's elbow this time.

"He's right, though. I did everything I could to keep him away." She smiled at him, a genuine smile. "But he's persistent."

"Come on," Jake told her. "You're glad I pushed, aren't you?"

"Yes." Keira squeezed Jake's hand. "I am." She nodded at Daniel. "We both are."

Touching, thought Elizabeth. All well and good for them, but what does that have to do with me?

"You're like me," said Keira. "I can tell."

From where Elizabeth sat, regarding Keira's punk-style spiked pixie cut hair, her torn jeans and combat boots, she could not see that they had anything in common other than meeting Jake and having sons who looked to be about the same age.

Keira started. "I'm a single mom."

"I guess I am too, now."

"My son has some issues."

"Mine, too." Where was this going?

Keira rustled her son's hair. "Daniel doesn't speak much."

"Neither does Timothy." So?

"I'm extremely protective of my son."

Elizabeth nodded. "I can understand that."

"My parents were furious when they found out I was pregnant out of wedlock."

"Oh, my parents were ecstatic at the thought of becoming grandparents. Sorry to hear about yours. That must have hurt."

"When they realized that the father had no plans to marry me, they disowned me."

How could parents do that? Then Elizabeth said, "Mine died." It just popped out.

Keira's eyes widened.

Elizabeth explained, "They were killed in an airplane accident just before Timothy was born."

"That's sad." At least Keira knew in some recess of her mind that her parents were still out there somewhere, even if they didn't want to see her or Daniel.

She changed the subject. Might as well get it all out there. "I don't have a good track record with men. The sperm donor ran off when he learned I was pregnant."

"Oh, I'm sorry. That's awful. Has he been involved since?"

"Nope, and we don't need him. Good riddance, as far we're concerned."

At least Jackson had been there for the birth then those first few years. Yeah, and look how had that ended. She could one-up Keira.

"My husband was here. At least until he tried to have me killed."

"Okay, you win. I can't top that one." Keira grinned.

Elizabeth could not help but grin back. What was humorous about this conversation? Why were they smiling at each other? They'd just bared their souls publicly to virtual strangers, and yet they were smiling? Bizarre. "Would you like some more coffee?"

As much as she had so not wanted company, they took her mind off worrying about which wounds Dr. Mayberry might want to pick at next.

Chapter Twelve

"How is he with animals?" Dr. Mayberry started this session with just Elizabeth, while Timothy remained in the inner waiting room, watched over by Doris. Elizabeth left the door ajar, she said, in case Timothy called for her. Dr. Mayberry raised her eyebrows. She'd not heard the child say one word yet.

"Ah, fine, I think. I'm not really sure. He hasn't been around animals at all, except for recently. He played with the neighbor's daughter and their little dog a few times now."

"Did he show fear of the animal? Panic? Any allergic reactions? Aggression?"

"No, he didn't seem afraid and no, he's never hurt an animal." Geez, what did this woman think her son was? "The first time he met the dog, the creature leapt on him. It only weighed maybe twenty pounds. They rolled on the floor together and both seemed to have a good time. Timothy hugged it, rather than trying to get away." She thought about allergies. "We suspected that Timothy might develop allergies; it's not uncommon in young children with seizure disorders. So far, we haven't really noticed anything. He has a narrow range of foods he prefers to eat, but we don't see any adverse reactions to any." Then she added, "Or rather, *I* don't see any. It's just me now, of course, but even before, it was mainly me paying attention to the details of Timothy's life." As if defending Jackson out of habit, "I was the stay-at-home parent, after all, and spent the most time with him."

"I see." She paused, long enough that Elizabeth looked uncomfortable. "That brings us to the topic of Jackson." Elizabeth didn't meet her gaze. "Why is it that a man who promised to love and honor you hired men to kill you?"

Elizabeth froze – both her body and her mind.

Dr. Mayberry continued to probe. "What was it about you that caused this utter twist in his feelings for you?"

Dr. Mayberry waited. Okay, too much, too soon. No point in driving her patient catatonic, at least not yet. She relented, and against her instincts, softened. "I know this is hard, beyond hard. But we'll need to look at these issues if we're to help your child. How about we let it go for now but consider this homework." She waited to see if her words were registering on Elizabeth. Reluctantly, the shrinking woman seemed to gather herself, and met Dr. Mayberry's gaze. "Over this next week, think about this." She held up her hand. "I know, I know, it's painful, both to consider what Jackson did to you and what part you might have played in this. But I want you to write down what Jackson did and what might have been behind his actions, and what you did and your motivations." She waited to see if those directions registered. "Can you do that for me?"

His turn. Elizabeth led Timothy by the hand into Dr.

Mayberry's office. He wiggled free from her grip and headed to the table where paints and an easel awaited.

"I guess he'll be okay with you then." Elizabeth's voice was tentative. After her gloves-off session with Dr. Mayberry, she needed time to herself. The psychologist had been nothing but kind to Timothy; surely it was all right to leave him in the doctor's care while she regrouped.

Giving her best reassuring smile, Dr. Mayberry nodded. She followed Elizabeth to the door and closed it behind the mother, leaving Timothy alone with her.

There were five pots of paint. Three had lids affixed loosely, the two on the right, near Timothy's dominant hand, and the last one on the left. The other two lids were more firmly screwed on. When Timothy hesitated, Dr. Mayberry said, "Go ahead and take the lids off. You are welcome to paint." He had success with the first one, then the second. He struggled with the third. She watched for three things - indications of how he would handle frustration, if he would give up and put the uncooperative ones aside, or if he would ask her for help.

He set the third pot back and picked up the fourth. After trying unsuccessfully to unscrew the lid, he turned his body to Dr. Mayberry. Without making eye contact, he brought the jar to her, holding it out. It was enough. They'd work on eye contact and making requests later. For now, he had reached out to her. She loosened the lid for him. He returned in a minute with the other one that had given him trouble. He waited patiently while she pretended to struggle, exaggerating her facial expression, and talking about how hard this one was to open.

The first time they tried painting, all the paint pot lids were open, the various colors on display. Timothy drew with only the black. With simple strokes, he drew a recognizable sofa with a coffee table in front of it, both pointed at a small television. Off to the side was a single chair.

When she had shared the picture with Elizabeth privately, Elizabeth's indrawn breath showed she recognized the images. Timothy's artistic skill belied his years. Elizabeth explained that that looked like the setup in the living room of the house where they were held when abducted. She wondered why her son would draw such a thing.

"This might be his way of processing what happened." Dr. Mayberry tilted her head to the side. "Have you talked to him about it?"

Elizabeth shook her head. "We've tried to put it behind us."

"Is that working? For you? For him?"

"For me, and probably for Timothy, I'm pretty sure. As you can see, we don't exactly hold conversations."

"No, at least not yet. But he doesn't need to talk back for you to converse with him. Talking to him is good for his language development." She let the rest drop, planning to return to the whole "put-it-behind-us-thing" later.

"I talk to him all the time," insisted Elizabeth.

"What does your talking consist of? Reading to him? Telling him what you want him to do?"

"Yes, both. I read to him every night before bed, and often in the afternoon before his nap. A couple of times he's brought me a book when he wants me to read to him."

Dr. Mayberry nodded and waited.

"And, of course, I tell him what I want him to do. I also give him some warning before we need to leave home. If I ask him too abruptly to stop what he's doing, I get resistance, or he drags his feet. But things go more smoothly with a five-minute warning."

"What else do you talk to him about?"

"As I said, he's really not much of a conversationalist. And besides, he's only four."

"Listening to language will encourage his understanding and use of language. Try talking aloud. Describe what you're doing while you wash the dishes or make supper. Describe aloud what you see him doing and elaborate on it." At Elizabeth's puzzled look, she gave an example. "Timothy, you're pushing the car. It's a red car and you're making it go fast. Is it faster than the green one?"

"Okay, I guess I could try that." There would be no one around to hear her, at least, so they wouldn't think she was talking to herself.

"And next time you come, we'll address some of those issues you're 'putting behind you'. We'll begin with some of the reasons your husband wanted you dead."

That had been last week. Hopefully, Elizabeth had talked more to this child in the interval.

Timothy's turn. Now, for something different.

Dr. Mayberry went to another door, one painted to match the walls of her office. She crouched down after opening the door. A purring sound started immediately. The psychologist rose with a Persian cat in her arms. She sat down on the couch; the cat circled her lap twice before getting off to sit beside her mistress. Her purrs began again. While she stroked the fine fur, Dr. Mayberry waited for Timothy to notice. At first, his hand stilled, then continued with the paintbrush. Several seconds later, he paused again. This time he turned around. His eyes scanned the environment, not in alarm, but in curiosity. Spying this recent addition to the room, he approached, paintbrush pointed to the ceiling.

"How about I hold that, little man?" Dr. Mayberry withdrew the brush from Timothy's grasp, and he let her take it, his attention elsewhere. A ceramic tray became the brush's repository where it could do no harm to furniture or clothing.

Cautiously, Timothy came closer, brushing in between Dr. Mayberry's knees and the coffee table. Good, he didn't mind contact with her, choosing that approach rather than the longer route around the other side of the table.

He observed the slumbering cat and the hand stroking the fur. Tentatively, he raised a hand, but didn't touch.

"That's fine, Timothy. You may pet her. Isn't her fur soft?"

One index finger got closer and closer until it touched the cat's side, then withdrew. That finger went into his mouth as he contemplated his next move. His whole hand reached out this time and he rested his palm flat on the cat's back, some of his saliva puddling in the fur. The cat's purring intensified. Timothy's small hand rested near where the psychologist stroked her cat's head and neck. Dr. Mayberry picked up Timothy's fingers and ran them down the sleek fur. She did it once, twice, then a third time until the little hand repeated the motion on their own. He glanced up at her, really looked into her eyes. He smiled.

Yes, this had potential, mused Dr. Mayberry. A vague longing morphed from an idea into the beginning of a plan.

Chapter Thirteen

"What would you think if I told Timothy to call me Hanna? Or Dr. M?"

Elizabeth was unsure how to respond to the psychologist's question. "Is it important? It's not like Timothy is going to be calling you anything."

"Not yet, but he will. I have full confidence in that." She smiled, an expression Elizabeth couldn't quite interpret. "Dr. Mayberry is a bit of a mouthful, don't you think?"

"It is multi-syllabic, but, as you might have guessed, I'm not opposed to that. After all, the name I chose for my son has three syllables. *We* chose," she corrected. "And my given name has four syllables."

"Yes, it is rather long. What did your parents call you?"

Elizabeth frowned. "Elizabeth, of course. That's what they named me."

"They didn't have any cute pet names for you? Something a little less formal? Liz? Lizzie? Beth? Betty?"

"No, they always called me by my proper name. And they called my brother Jonathan."

"Hmmm."

Elizabeth was coming to dislike that combination of letters.

Changing the subject, Dr. Mayberry said, "Tell me more about Jonathan."

His death was not something Elizabeth enjoyed talking about. In her family, it was almost a taboo subject. After the funeral, by tacit consent, they all refrained from saying his name.

"He was three years older than me, almost four. I looked up to him." She thought back to those years. "Sometimes he tried to ignore me. I guess that was normal. He was twelve, and I was just nine. I couldn't keep up with him in the things he liked to do. But when he paid me some attention, it was nice. I adored him and wanted to please him."

"Did you?"

"Pardon me?"

"Did you please him?"

What an odd question. "I don't know. He treated me okay, at least at far as older brothers go, I believe."

"Where were you when the incident happened?"

Incident. Such an innocuous word for those few moments that transformed all their lives. "We were at the ocean. Daddy rented this cottage." Elizabeth thought back. "Mother called it a cottage, but really it was a house, a pretty pleasant house."

"Tell me about it."

"It had three bedrooms and a den where daddy worked much of the day. There was a kitchen, and a butler's pantry. Mother used that to get us drinks; Marcia was our cook. She came with us and spent time in the kitchen. She had a small suite off the kitchen where she stayed."

Dr. Mayberry nodded. "Sounds like a nice place."

"It was," Elizabeth agreed. "Smaller than our home, but just right for a summer holiday." She smiled. "We went there three summers in a row. We had some good times there."

"Who did you play with?"

"Mostly my brother. We didn't really make friends in the area, or my parents didn't. There were a few other kids on the beach some days, but they were mostly either a lot older than us or a lot younger. We weren't encouraged to socialize with others."

"Were you lonely?"

Elizabeth looked at her quizzically. The thought had never occurred to her. "No. No, I don't think so. We were used to being on our own or playing with the children of our parents' friends when they arranged play dates for us."

"Did that happen often?"

"Sometimes. Not every day, for sure. Not every week, either."

"So, that day there were just the two of you kids playing?"

"Yes. We went swimming. Marcia was supposed to be watching us from the kitchen window. It was a bay window over the sink and looked out on the ocean."

"Where were your parents?"

"Daddy was working in the den. He rarely took time off from work and always had lots to do."

"And your mother?"

"She was reading a book and napping in a lounge chair on the deck."

"You and your brother were on the beach?"

"Yes, for a while, and then we got hot. We had on our bathing suits, so we went into the water to cool off."

"I bet that felt nice."

Elizabeth closed her eyes. "Yes. Yes, it did. The ocean water at first was freezing on my skin after being overheated on the sand. But almost right away it felt good.

"Jonathan went in first; he always did that. While I'd stick in my toe, then creep in inch by inch, he took half a dozen lunging steps, then dove right under. None of that slowly getting used to it for him."

"Sounds like he enjoyed the water."

She nodded. "He was a decent swimmer. Excellent, even. That's why my parents didn't worry about us going into the water on our own. They knew how well Jonathan swam, and that he'd look after me." Her eyes filled, and she blinked several times. "He did. He did look after me."

"What happened next?"

"Jonathan went out deeper. I didn't like to go past where I could touch the bottom, but Jonathan never worried about that. He was a fish.

"I tried to keep up with him this time, and so went out deeper than I'd usually venture. It was okay. I was swimming, and it's easier to float in the salt water than in our pool at home.

"The sun felt good, and it was just the right temperature now that I'd gotten used to the water. I lay on my back floating, just enjoying the feel of the air and the ocean and the sun."

Dr. Mayberry waited.

"Then Jonathan shouted. My ears were under the water, so his words came through muffled. I straightened up to tread water so I could hear better. I couldn't see my brother. I spun in the water and couldn't see the shore, either. How had I gotten out so far?

"Then Jonathan's shouts came closer. He was making a lot of splashes as he swam toward me. When he was closer,

I could see the muscles in his shoulders straining. I wondered why he was swimming so hard. Then I noticed that although I was just treading water, he was swimming hard. I was still drifting farther away.

"He told me not to worry, that he'd get me. I'd be okay. He started yelling at me to swim to him. I'd never heard him use that tone of voice before. He wasn't teasing and he wasn't mocking. He seemed, well, scared. My big brother didn't get scared."

"What did you do?"

"I started swimming to him as hard as I could; I wasn't a great swimmer." She added, "But I'm better now. I've worked at it so that this would never happen again."

"What happened next?"

"We made some progress in getting closer to one another. Jonathan kept yelling, 'Swim across it. Don't fight the current. Come to me.' Then he kept hollering about riptide. I didn't know what that was.

"Finally, our fingers touched, and he grabbed onto me. He pushed me to the side and yelled to swim as hard as I could. When I hesitated, he said he'd be right behind me. Then he pushed me harder, and I torpedoed through the water. Or that's what it felt like. He said to get to shore and get dad. When I turned my head to look back at him, he waved his arm and said to go, go fast. He needed me to get dad."

Elizabeth brushed a tear from her cheek, but others followed its track immediately. "My brother never needed me for anything. *I* was the one who always needed help. So, this one time he asked me for something, I would do it. I swam as hard as I could. When I had no breath left, I kept going.

"I was fairly close to shore when I heard voices calling

my name. When I looked up, Marcia and my mother were there, both wading into the water with their clothes on. They pulled me the rest of the way to the beach. Their faces were all wet. I thought they'd gone under the water, too, but later realized that they were crying.

"Daddy was there. He was launching the canoe and paddling faster than I'd ever seen him move. He hollered at mother to go get help." She looked at Dr. Mayberry. "Daddy never raised his voice and definitely not at mother. That's when I knew that something was really wrong. Something bad."

"Was it as bad as you thought?"

Elizabeth nodded. "Worse. Daddy canoed way out, so far that we couldn't see him anymore. Then other boats came, motorboats that sailed back and forth, in and out."

"Do you know what happened?"

"I didn't at the time, but I learned about it later. A riptide had come up. They can come out of nowhere. While I was floating on my back, I got caught in one, not even realizing that I was being pulled out to sea. My brother noticed and tried to get me. He did, like he said he would. When he pushed me, he got sucked in the riptide and it must have gotten stronger. It pulled him out to sea quickly. Daddy and the other boats stayed out all night looking. Light beams were all over the water and klaxons sounded for hours, but they never found him."

She reached for a tissue. "That was the last time I saw my brother. The last that anyone saw of him."

Chapter Fourteen

Exhausted, Elizabeth changed places with Timothy, allowing his turn with the psychologist. She buried her face behind a magazine, not up to exchanging courtesies with Doris, no matter how pleasant the woman tried to be. She glanced at her watch. Unbelievable! She had only been in there for forty-five minutes, but it felt like she'd had a marathon session with Dr. Mayberry. To top it off, the psychologist had asked her if she wanted to discuss her homework with her. No!

Is that what it was like for Timothy? It couldn't be. He was just a child. Although he'd had some recent trauma, his young brain wouldn't understand the intricacies of what had happened. She was sure he'd put it out of his mind, just as her parents told her to do all those years ago.

"Welcome, Timothy. What would you like to do today?" She had several stations set up for him - paints, paper and crayons, a dollhouse, and a kitchen. Last time, she had given him two options. He'd seemed hesitant and more comfortable when she suggested he try one first. Today, she wanted to leave it up to him, see how he handled the indecision, how long he would stick with one activity, and if he would stick to the known or be willing to explore.

Instead, he settled on nothing. Flitting wasn't really the word for a sedate child like Timothy, but he appeared restless. He picked up a paintbrush and put it down, he sat momentarily in front of the dollhouse but didn't touch it. Between each thing that held his interest, he glanced at her and at her lap. What was he searching for?

"Timothy, is there something you want?" Words were not the only way to communicate. Would he show her?

He moved past the coffee table to lean against her knees. His hand stroked the couch beside her, then her thigh, then back to the couch. His fingers went into his mouth and he looked at her.

"Ah, I think I know what you want, little man." She pointed to the far wall. "See that door over there? Open it and I think you'll find what you're after."

Good. He could follow her point. He tried turning the doorknob. It wasn't really a knob that required turning. It was a latch that responded to an easy pull.

"Try again. Use both hands."

Timothy complied, and the door came open in his hands. Then he disappeared inside.

Seconds later, he returned, following Honey, the cat. Honey leapt onto the couch. She turned a circle, then settled in with a purr. Timothy knelt on the floor in front of the couch, at first just watching the cat. Then, tentatively, one finger reached out. He glanced at the psychologist, as if asking permission.

"Yes, you may pet her." Still, he hesitated. "Like this,"

Dr. Mayberry demonstrated. "Stroke her the way her fur grows. Just gently, now." Timothy hardly needed that reminder, and his touch gentled naturally. When he took his hand away, the purring stopped, and Honey opened an eye to look at him. As if that was the signal to continue, Timothy began his petting again, and the purring resumed.

This was a good time for the introduction, the next phase of their therapy. "You stay right there and look after Honey, Timothy. I'll be right back with a surprise."

Returning, she sat on the couch and put one of two sets of headphones over her ears. Her face became relaxed and happy. She closed her eyes for half a minute, pretending to enjoy what she was hearing. "Do you want a try?" she asked Timothy.

He looked only slightly interested; the cat was more important.

Gently, she took the second, smaller set of headphones and placed them on Timothy's head. Using a remote, she increased the volume of the Gregorian music just slightly, not enough to demand the child's full attention, but enough so he could hear it. His eyes registered that he heard, but he did not remove the headset. They'd go easy today, just listening to the music for a bit, while enjoying the sensory aspects of cuddling with Honey.

Dr. Mayberry led Timothy to the inner waiting, settled him with some crayons and paper and asked him to draw a picture of Honey. She motioned for Elizabeth to come back to the office with her.

Once seated, she handed Elizabeth the headphones that Timothy had worn. "Try them on, please." Elizabeth's head looked small enough to fit them. Not quite, though. Elizabeth resized them until she could put them on. Dr. Mayberry's remote started the music softly.

"This is Gregorian music. Timothy spent about half an hour listening to this today. I'd like you to take these headphones home and have him work up to listening for several hours a day. He'll listen to this and other music I'll provide."

"Why?"

"We're starting what is known as auditory integration therapy. We know that your son can hear - he follows directions well. But hearing is a passive activity whereby we receive auditory information through the ear.

"But listening is more involved. We want Timothy to not just hear, but to listen actively - to focus, filter, respond to and remember sound. There is evidence to show that this type of auditory training aids in language development for some children."

Elizabeth's eyes widened. "It could make him talk?"

"*Make* him is not the word I would use. We're hoping that it will encourage language development, making it easier for him to communicate expressively."

"What will he be listening to?"

"Mainly Gregorian-type chants type music and Mozart. These emphasize high-frequency sounds, which seem to work best in auditory integration therapy."

"He's only four. How am I going to convince him to sit still for several hours and just listen?" He was a reasonably obedient child, but even he had his limits.

"That's the beauty of this approach. He does not need to alter what he is doing. He can wear the headphones while he's playing or eating or riding in the car. In fact, it's good to have his hands busy at the same time. Ideally, we'll work up to four hours of listening a day."

Elizabeth looked unconvinced.

"What can it hurt? He tolerated the headset well today. I'll give you a remote control; we had the volume on number four today. I'll also give you charger so you can plug the headphones in overnight."

"How long before we see a difference in him?"

"Ah, if I had the answer to that, I'd make a fortune in predicting winnings. No one knows. Everybody responds differently and in their own time. He's young, so that's a plus. He's also been through trauma, so his brain may take longer to heal and respond."

"Okay, we'll try."

"Excellent. I'll see you next week."

Yes, excellent. Ideas were forming in the psychologist's mind. She had plans for this child.

"Bitz! Bitz!" Timothy stood at the front window, palms flat and banging on the glass. "Bitz!"

Elizabeth put her pen down. Was that her imagination, or had Timothy spoken? She listened.

"Bitz!" He banged on the window with his open hands.

"Bitz? What on earth did he mean? Great. Just great. The first word he had spoken in months and it wasn't mommy. It wasn't even anything she could understand.

Timothy turned to her and banged on the window again. "Bitz!"

She joined him, looking at their front lawn. To the left, Cynthia was holding the car door for Amy. Crawling into the vehicle with her was their dog, Blitz. Oh, Bitz meant Blitz.

"Yes, Timothy, there's Blitz." She remembered Dr Mayberry's advice to repeat Timothy's words and expand on them. "And there's Amy and her mom, Cynthia." She corrected herself, "I mean, Mrs. Blythe."

Cynthia's head turned in their direction. "Shall we wave to them?"

Cynthia waved in return and a smaller hand moved back and forth from the car seat in the back seat.

It took a dog to make her son say his first word. Well, she'd take it, no matter the cause. Hopefully, where one word was, there'd be more.

And there was. By no means was there a torrent, but there were a few. "No" was one of them. Oh, joy - the terrible twos starting when he was almost five. But words were words.

At lunch, when she set his milk in front of Timothy, he shoved it back and said, "juice". Well. He'd always been a kid who went along with whatever. Today, she'd indulge him. If the boy wanted juice and even asked for it, he could have it. It would have been nice to have a "please" with it, though. They'd work on it.

She'd hoped that once he spoke one word, the dam would burst and all the words he'd been hoarding inside would tumble out. No, it didn't work that way, apparently.

"Ms. Whitmore? Hello, I'm Nancy Grey. I'm a speech/language pathologist. Dr. Muller sent me a referral for your son, Timothy."

Elizabeth had forgotten about that referral. They had started it long before all the craziness came into their lives.

"I realize that you've been on the waiting list for some time, and I apologize for that. We have a cancellation next week, Wednesday afternoon at two o'clock. Would that be convenient for you?"

Convenient? That depended. Good thing there was a few week's hiatus from court. It felt like she was running to appointments non-stop. What was one more? Right, she thought. One more stranger probing into their lives.

After taking down the address and exchanging insurance information, Elizabeth hung up the phone. With a sigh, she added the appointment into her phone's calendar app. More interfering people to contend with.

Chapter Fifteen

Like the playroom at the courthouse, this room in the speech/language pathologist's office held child-sized furniture and muted colors. There were shelves closed off with taupe curtains, although what looked like a puppet theatre stood off on its own.

Nancy Grey brought Timothy some large wooden puzzles. Each piece had a handle. After Timothy quickly completed the six-piece ones, she replaced them with more complex puzzles.

The door opened and a smiling young woman joined them at the table.

"Hi! Timothy, I'd like you to meet Tammy. Tammy, this is Timothy and his mom, Elizabeth."

Tammy held out her hand to Timothy.

Elizabeth held her breath. Would her son be rude?

At first, Timothy did not glance up from his puzzle. Tammy didn't withdraw her hand.

"Timothy, Tammy wants to shake your hand." She put

a gentle finger on his upper arm, guiding him towards the outstretched hand.

Timothy's hand met Tammy's unerringly. How did he do that without appearing to look? He immediately returned to his puzzle.

Tammy rose and extended her hand to Elizabeth. "Nice to meet you," she said, "I'll be playing with your son while you two talk." When she smiled, the light caught the braces on her lower teeth.

Elizabeth froze. How old was this person? How could she leave Timothy with this child? No. Just no.

Nancy touched her arm and pointed to the mirror that took up much of one wall. She pointed to Timothy, then the mirror and whispered, "Come with me. You can come back in a second if you feel you need to."

Watching Tammy join Timothy at the puzzles, she told him, "Mommy will be right back."

Timothy gave no sign that he heard or noticed her leaving.

Nancy led Elizabeth to the next door in the hallway and flipped on the indirect lights. She motioned Elizabeth toward the window with her. It was a one-way mirror and on the other side, Timothy and Tammy were clearly visible. He seemed content. "As long as we speak softly, we can observe, and he likely won't know that we're in here watching."

"I take it you've done this often. Do you have a lot of nervous parents?" Elizabeth doubted she'd be the only one reluctant to leave her child alone with a stranger.

"I'm not sure nervous is the word I'd use. Interested. I work a lot with preschoolers and it's important to have the caregivers involved. They, after all, are the primary therapists."

That was a novel idea to Elizabeth. So far, all the professionals she'd come across seemed to think that Timothy required people other than his mother to help him.

Nancy continued. "We like to have the parents involved in every aspect of what we do. That's why we have this mirror, so moms like you can observe what we're doing.

For all her apparent youth, Tammy seemed good with Timothy. He didn't mind her presence and allowed her to take turns putting the puzzle together. Nancy flipped a switch on the wall and Tammy's words filled the room.

"One-way speaker," Nancy explained.

They finished the puzzle, all but for one piece. Tammy held the last piece in the air beside her face and watched Timothy as he searched the table, then the floor underneath. "Timothy, is this what you're looking for?" As soon as Timothy raised his eyes, she held out the piece for him. "This is the final piece. Good job on completing this puzzle. Do you want to do another one?"

No reply.

Tammy waited. She looked as if she had all the time in the world. Finally, Timothy glanced at her. She immediately pulled out two puzzles from where they rested on her lap. She thrust the one in her right hand forward. "Do you want this one?" Now she moved the one in her left hand closer to Timothy. "Or this one?" Again, she waited with an expectant smile on her face. No pressure, just time.

"Why doesn't she just give him one?" Elizabeth asked. "He might get frustrated."

Nancy turned to her. "A little frustration is all right. We all experience it, and need to get used to how it feels, and how to handle those emotions." She nodded at Tammy. "The other thing she's working on is how to make choices, which is another skill we all need."

"I could guess which one he'd prefer."

"I'm sure that you could. You've probably become adept at anticipating his needs."

Elizabeth nodded.

"When we're trying to develop Timothy's communication skills, we might need to wait. Even if we *think* we know what he wants, we need to let him show us."

"But he doesn't talk."

"His speech is certainly the goal. Speech is the generally the fastest and most efficient way of getting across our wants and needs. But until he's talking freely, there are other ways to communicate." She nodded at the window. "Let's watch. If we don't jump in too quickly, usually the child will find a way to let us know his preference."

Elizabeth prided herself on her efficiency. Why waste time when there was a lot to get done? Tammy, though, had infinite patience. She simply held the two puzzles out. Finally, after what seemed like forever to the anxious mother, Timothy raised his eyes to the puzzle on the right.

Nancy grinned as if Timothy had achieved something major. Maybe he had, but Elizabeth didn't get it.

"Elizabeth? Hi, it's Cynthia. Sorry we couldn't stop and talk yesterday when Timothy waved. We were late for an appointment at the dog groomers."

Dog groomer. After seeing Timothy's reaction to Dr. Mayberry's cat and how he played with Amy's little dog, it had crossed Elizabeth's mind that maybe they should get a pet. Then, after Timothy spoke Blitz's name, the idea took root. But a dog groomer? Just how much work was it to have an animal?

"If you'll pardon my asking, what exactly does a dog groomer do?"

"It depends on the breed. Ones like my Blitz have hair that continues to grow, so he needs a trim. Ideally, I should take him every month where he's bathed and clipped, but sometimes I let it slide."

Hmm. Every month.

"Anyway, I've just put some chocolate chip cookies in the oven. When they come out, I don't want to be tempted to eat them all. Would you and Timothy come over and keep us from devouring the entire batch on our own?"

Elizabeth looked at Timothy, on his stomach, half-heartedly pushing his train across the floor, making sounds with his lips. This isn't how he'd looked when he played with Amy. Or with Daniel, for that matter. Maybe he did need some kid time.

Elizabeth was not used to spur-of-the-moment social gatherings. Growing up, activities were planned and scheduled, not spontaneous. But her schedule for the afternoon held nothing that could not be put off until this evening. Why not? "Sure." It came out before she fully thought of the ramifications. Did she truly *want* to become closer to this woman? Possibly, if she was going to use her baby-sitting services once court started up again. She seemed like an agreeable person and Timothy enjoyed being with Amy, but still. She wasn't really seeking friendships for herself. Maybe for Timothy's sake, though. "When do you want us and what should I bring?"

When she told Timothy where they were going, his eyes glowed in a way she'd not seen in a while. Without needing a five-minute warning, he sat down by the door to put on his shoes. Yes, this had been the right decision. Just because she was not overly social did not mean that she should restrict Timothy's friendships as well.

The smells of melting chocolate filled the air as soon as Elizabeth opened the door in response to a yelled "Come in" from Cynthia. No one appeared right away to welcome them to Elizabeth helped Timothy off with his jacket and set his shoes on the tray by the door, alongside a little girl's pink runners. The lack of a greeting filled Elizabeth with unease. That would never have happened in her home - either the one she shared with Jackson or in her parents' home. You went to the door to welcome guests, and certainly, guests did not just walk into your home on their own.

"Sorry about that," a rushed Cynthia called from the upstairs landing. "We had a little mishap, but we're fine now."

"Is everything okay?"

"Amy was a bit too eager when I took the cookie sheet from the oven. She burnt her finger and got melted chocolate on the front of her shirt." She held up Amy's bandaged finger. "All fine." She led them into the kitchen. "The cookies should be cool enough now." To Timothy, "You ready for some, Bud?"

He pointed to himself. "Timothy." He waited.

Cynthia smiled and acknowledged him. "Timothy," she repeated. "But I still might call you Bud sometimes." She ruffled his hair.

Elizabeth watched the easy interaction. The two times Timothy had spoken recently were both in connection to this family. She didn't know what to make of that, other than that they might need to see more of them.

After Cynthia used wet paper towels to wipe off two

milk mustaches and four chocolatey hands, the kids raced off to the other room.

"Should we go with them?" Elizabeth was unused to Timothy being out of her sight.

"Nah, they're fine. We can hear them from here. Amy knows what she can and cannot touch. I'm sure they're pulling out toys, and there won't be room to step on the floor." She took a sip of her coffee, then refilled both of their mugs. "Thank you for dropping everything and coming over. I really appreciate it."

"Thank you for inviting us."

"As you can probably guess, the cookies were just an excuse."

Elizabeth had thought little about the reason behind the invitation.

"This is a rough day for me. Amy doesn't know the date, but it's two years ago today that Todd died." She seemed intrigued by the swirls the cream made as she stirred it into her coffee. "I know it should be getting easier, but sometimes it's not. Most of the time I'm okay, but today, I just didn't want to be alone." She looked across at Elizabeth. "You know what I mean?"

Not entirely sure that their loss was comparable, Elizabeth nodded. It seemed the right thing to do.

Cynthia continued. "I know that this is the way it is and that I'm a single parent now, but sometimes, just sometimes, I'm scared. I think about how hard it is, how hard it will be as Amy gets older, and I need to be both mother and father to her.

"At least when Todd was here, we could spell each other off if I got tired. We usually both didn't get frustrated at the same time and knew when to let the other take over. But now, it's just me and I worry that I don't always get it right."

When was the last time someone had spoken so intimately to Elizabeth? Almost never, or at least not since college when she and some of her sorority sisters had stayed up late talking. Those times had made Elizabeth slightly uncomfortable, but, on the other hand, she'd felt part of those girls' lives.

Cynthia looked like she was waiting for her to respond. Before she could think too much about it, or censure what came out of her mouth, Elizabeth offered, "Maybe we can spell each other off sometimes."

From the relief on Cynthia's face, it was the right thing to say. And, to Elizabeth too, it felt right.

Chapter Sixteen

This time Tammy was waiting for them in the playroom when Elizabeth and Timothy arrived at the speech therapy office. Timothy's expression didn't change, but he willingly reached for Tammy's outstretched hand and settled in front of the oversized easel with her. He didn't seem perturbed when Nancy explained that she and mommy would be next door.

Elizabeth and Nancy settled into the easy chairs facing the one-way mirror, watching Tammy introduce Timothy to finger-painting. Although his eyes followed each of Tammy's movements and messy smears on the paper, so far, he'd not been enticed to get his hands dirty.

"That might be my fault," explained Elizabeth. "I've never introduced Timothy to anything like finger-painting."

"There's no 'fault' to it. We're trying to see how he responds to different things. Look," she nodded to the window. "He's intrigued. I wouldn't be surprised if he joined in."

Tammy took two plastic gloves from a nearby box and slipped them onto her hands. She dipped her gloved fingers into a paint pot and smeared the colors onto the paper. She turned to Timothy and smiled, holding out the box of gloves. "Want some?"

She held the box there - just out of Timothy's reach. She waited. And waited. Timothy reached for the box. "Would you like some gloves, Timothy?"

"Yes," came his reply.

Nancy fist-pumped the air. "Yes! Way to go, Timothy!"

Elizabeth's smile was more guarded. "He's spoken several times this week," she said. "Each time is with someone other than me."

Nancy waited for her to explain.

"The first time was when he saw the neighbor's dog, Blitz. He said, 'Bitz' over and over, and tried to get their attention." She watched Timothy struggle to get the gloves on. Indicating her son, she said, "Shouldn't Tammy help him?" Even as she said the words, Timothy's concentrated expression turned to triumph as he completed his task and dipped one tentative finger into the black paint then dabbed at the paper.

"Guess not," said Nancy. "It's good for him to struggle a bit and acquire a new skill." She hastened to add, "Tammy would not have let it get out of hand though. She has good instincts about when to push and when to step in. Besides," she added, "you were right here and would know if it was time to intervene."

Elizabeth wasn't so sure about that. Did she rush in to do things for Timothy too quickly? More to think about. She continued her story. "Then, when we were next door visiting, the neighbor called him 'Bud'. Timothy corrected her, clearly saying that he was 'Timothy'."

"Excellent!"

"And, at the psychologist's he said 'cat'." She explained that Dr. Mayberry kept a cat in her office and Timothy enjoyed petting it.

"Animals can be soothing creatures. Even just stroking fur can meet sensory needs and have a calming effect. Plus, animals are often responsive to even small overtures."

"I've wondered if we should get a pet, if it would be good for Timothy."

"It might be. A dog or cat can bring big changes into a home though, if you're not used to having them around."

Elizabeth nodded. That part worried her.

"Why does he only speak sometimes? It's not that he's mute - he can form words, and when he was younger, he spoke more."

"From the oral-motor exam I did, I don't see any mechanical reason he isn't speaking. He seems to have the physical structures in place. He had the muscle control to at least roughly imitate my mouth movements."

"Dr. Muller, his pediatric neurologist, thinks that since there's been seizure activity in the left frontal-temporal areas that Broca's area might have been affected, impeding his language production."

"Could be. His receptive language seems intact, which is positive."

"So, if he can hear and understand what he hears, why doesn't he talk like other four-year-olds?"

"Good question. There are some reasons I think we can rule out. One is a hearing impairment; if a child cannot hear spoken language, then he has no models to imitate. Another common reason is an intellectual disability. While I don't see any formal assessment in his file, just from observing his actions and interactions, they seem within typical limits for his age, and he appears to have met other milestones appropriately, so likely he does not have a global developmental delay. Kids who are autistic sometimes experience language delays. Or, as Dr. Muller suggested, the seizures might have slowed down his language skills.

"But let's look at the good news."

Elizabeth stuck on the word 'autistic'.

Nancy continued. "It is more concerning if a child has both a receptive and expressive language delay. I've not formally assessed him yet, but from our observations, he seems to process what he hears well enough to follow directions and to make choices.

"Another good sign is that he used gestures." At Elizabeth's puzzled expression, she explained. "The words we use only convey part of what we want to get across. We use facial expressions, body language, and gestures to reinforce or take the place of words. We've seen Timothy point and use other gestures to get what he wants. That's excellent.

"The other encouraging fact is that he has spoken in the past and he is speaking now." As Elizabeth started to interrupt, she held up her hand. "I know, I know, it's not as frequent as you would like, but it's coming. In just the past weeks you say that he's gone from saying nothing at all to saying a word occasionally. And he used those words appropriately."

"Why can he do it sometimes, but not at other times?" Shouldn't it be an all-or-nothing skill?

"When you or I speak, it's automatic. We don't think about it. But for some kids, even though the words might be in their mind, they don't just automatically come out. We're learning more about this from autistic adults who are at times minimally verbal. They describe how, especially under times of stress, that the words just won't come out, seeming trapped in their mind."

"Are you suggesting that Timothy's autistic?"

"I don't know."

Well, that wasn't reassuring. Elizabeth watched her son. Both gloved hands were now lathered in multi-colored hues as he swirled his fingers across a fresh sheet of paper, his smile wide. Tammy raised a finger from her own paper and touched a bright, blue finger to Timothy's nose.

He froze.

Tammy grabbed a nearby hand-held mirror and moved it in front of Timothy's face. His blue nose filled the space.

Eyes wide, he looked from the mirror to Tammy. Then, while the women watched, he placed one mucky gloved hand on the back of a wooden chair to steady himself as he climbed up to stand on the seat. He reached out a finger and painted Tammy's nose.

Elizabeth sucked in a breath. What had her son done?

"Ew, gross," laughed Tammy.

"Gross," echoed Timothy.

Tears came to Elizabeth's eyes.

"Hi, Murph." Dr. Hanna Mayberry settled herself into Dr. Arnold Murphy's leather couch, kicking off her shoes, and pulling her feet up beside her.

"Hello, Hanna. Good to see you. How are things going?"

"Remember that new client I told you about? I think this is really going somewhere."

"You're jazzed about this one."

"You got that right."

"Sometimes in our line of work, it can seem that clients are repetitions of one another."

"Occupational hazard. But not this one."

"Tell me about it."

"It's mainly the child who intrigues me. There's this curiosity behind his silent eyes."

"Silent?"

"He's nonverbal. Or at least he has been for the past while. I'm not getting a clear picture from the mother just how verbal he was at one time, but it seems that his expressive language development stopped at some point, apart from the odd vocalization. Then, even those sounds stopped after he went through trauma."

"What sort of trauma?"

"I'll come back to the language part in a moment."

Murph nodded. Over the years they'd worked out their own ways of getting through a story.

"This kid has been through a lot, although it sounds like he had a reasonably solid family life prior to that. I'll have a better handle on that after I've had a few more sessions with the mother.

"Anyway, his mother stopped for gas, leaving her son sleeping in the back seat of the car." She shook her head. "I know we're not supposed to make judgements about our clients but still…. While the mom was in paying for the gas, she spied this guy getting in her car and starting to drive."

At Murph's raised eyebrows, she added, "Yes, the keys were left in the ignition." She continued the story. "The mom drops her things and runs to the car, throwing herself inside the back seat as this guy drives off. She can't convince him to let them out somewhere, even though all he wanted was her car; he hadn't noticed the boy in the back seat. He kept them for almost a week, holing up at his grandmother's old place, then he got nervous and went on the run with them. It ended in a hotel room."

"Where were the police in all this? The family?"

"That's the interesting part. Apparently, the father and his girlfriend wanted rid of the mom but wanted her money. They hired someone to kidnap, then do away with her. When the police became suspicious of hubby, that threw them, because the trail went cold. This was actually a random snatch, despite a real one being in the works."

"Are we talking a lot of money here, enough for the husband to risk so much?"

"By the average person's standards, it'd likely be a nice chunk of change, certainly enough to not have to work ever again. They lived well. The house they were in was a gift from her parents. There was plenty of money in her trust fund, but she was tight with those purse strings. Hubby wanted more than his salary brought in."

"How'd they get away?"

"I don't have all the details yet, but the mother finally got desperate enough to take some action. The police were also closing in by then, as was the husband, so things came together near the end. But not before the mother took a bullet to the shoulder, and the kidnapper's still in hospital."

"And the husband?"

"He's in remand waiting for his turn in court."

"How's the child taking it?"

Hanna narrowed her eyes. "I'm not sure. On the surface, he seems to cope and is settling back into his old life. I've not heard of him asking for his father, but his dad was often away on business.

"Medically, the child is stable now. He has a seizure disorder and was without his medication for the time someone abducted them. The report from his neurologist is optimistic."

"The good news is," continued Hanna, "that over the past week, he's spoken a few words. Not lots, but it's a start."

"Do you trust the mother's reporting on this?"

"I question some of her observations or lack of observations, but my instincts say that she's telling the truth when she reports that he used some words. The descriptions of the circumstances surrounding these incidents seem too detailed to be confabulation. Plus, I heard him say 'cat' in my office."

"Ah, Honey. Has that cat worked her magic again?"

"Apparently. I doubt that this child's hand has ever stroked a cat before, but he is intrigued with her."

"To what do you attribute his utterances?"

She grinned at her old friend and therapist. "Me, of course."

Murph gave an eye roll worthy of any teenager.

"Here's what I think's happening," began Hanna. "First, the mom is starting to open up to me. She had some earlier experiences that taught her to keep everything inside; that was encouraged by her parents, and I think she's done the same with Timothy."

"Is evidence of his trauma coming through in therapy?"

"No, not yet. I didn't want the mom to rabbit on me, so I'm working on the thing that means the most to her first - having her son speak.

"He's now seeing a speech/language pathologist; that started a few weeks ago. We've worked on trust, and the child seems comfortable with me now. Prior to this, he has rarely left his mom's side, and has certainly not been alone with another adult.

"I've recently started Auditory Integration with him."

"You think that is wise." One of Murph's famous questions phrased as a statement.

Elizabeth played along. "To answer your question, yes, in this instance I do. It will serve my purpose."

"*Your* purpose?"

"Yes, as part of my plan to move him to where I want him to be."

Chapter Seventeen

Elizabeth hummed as she prepared lunch. She stopped and checked herself in the mirror over the sink. Yes, she looked better. Those lines in her forehead had smoothed out. That constant tension in the back of her neck wasn't there. She could not remember the last time she had sung or hummed. Maybe life was settling into its new normal.

The words, "Go, go, go!" came from the other room. Timothy and his train engines. His words were more frequent now. Oh, not where she'd like them to be, but she heard utterances more and more often. Dr. Mayberry's Auditory Integration Training was a godsend.

Timothy ran into the kitchen and barrelled into her, wrapping his arms around her legs. This was another change - a more affectionate child. She hugged him back, swinging them from side to side. "Almost ready for lunch, little man?"

"Noodles," came his reply.

Noodles, in fact, any kind of pasta was not allowed on

his ketogenic diet. It had been ages since she'd given him any. How did he even remember?

She looked into her son's upturned, smiling face. How could she resist him? This child who had been through so much, had lost so much, was asking her for something so simple. His diet was in place in an effort to reduce his seizures, but it had been weeks since he'd had a tonic-clonic episode; she could not remember when she last witnessed him having an absence seizure.

The last time she asked Dr. Muller, he said that the only way to know if the reduced seizure activity was because of the medications or the diet was to eliminate one of these variables. He strongly advised against tinkering with the meds since it had taken so long to get them right. That left just this diet. Although she was happy to continue it if it was necessary for Timothy's health, the dietary restrictions were truly a pain.

And she had already slipped up. She thought of the chocolate chip cookies Timothy had consumed at Cynthia's house. At the time, it didn't even occur to her to restrict what he was sampling; he was just a child enjoying the gooey, warm treat. That indulgence had not brought on any seizures.

"Sure, noodles coming right up." If he would actually *say* the word for what he wanted, how could she refuse him?

While she wouldn't abandon the carb-free diet for him totally just yet, the odd bit of cheating might not hurt. Besides, she wouldn't mind a plate of pasta herself, preferably baked with a tangy, cheesy sauce. Oh, what would her mother say about such indulgent, fattening food? Elizabeth smiled to herself. While her mother had kept strict control over her family's caloric intake, maybe it was okay to loosen up sometimes.

Punctuality was ingrained in Elizabeth. It was a sign of respect, both for her own time and that of other people. Not too early, as that made you look anxious, but with enough time to allow for anything unexpected that might crop up (such as getting kidnapped, she thought).

The letter written on Judge Bursey's stationery requested her presence in his office at ten o'clock. Fifteen minutes before the hour found Elizabeth and Timothy waiting on the bench in the hallway by the inner chambers. While waiting with her son used to be no problem, lately Timothy had shown more energy; he was less inclined to sit passively with a toy. Today, Elizabeth resorted to the electronic babysitter, the iPad. She used to frown at the notion of parents using electronics to keep their child quiet, but recently she had relaxed her stance on that type of pacifier.

"The Judge will see you now."

As Elizabeth reached for her son's arm, he pulled back and made a protesting sound. "Paw, Paw." Even without the full sentence, it was clear that he wanted to continue watching this episode of Paw Patrol. Since getting to know their neighbor's dog, this was his favorite show. If he had to be stuck on something, there were worse shows for kids, though. But just not now.

"He's okay there. I'll watch him if you like." The receptionist pointed to a chair near her desk. "Leave him here with me."

Elizabeth glanced at her son, torn. She knew that the Judge would not be pleased to see Timothy with her, but today she had had no choice. He also criticized her lack of trust in others and clinging to her son. Maybe this would be okay. Who should be more trustworthy than someone working directly for a federal judge? She decided. "Thank you so much. That would really help. Would you mind if I left the door open just a bit? Then I can hear if he needs me."

The receptionist waved her into the inner office. "Sure, that's fine. We'll be here waiting for you."

"Good day, Ms. Whitmore. I see that you came alone today."

"Not exactly, Your Honor. My son's in that room," she indicated over her shoulder, "with your receptionist." She hurried to add, "He won't bother her; he's watching a movie and won't interfere with her work."

"I'm glad you'll entrust him with my staff. Baby steps, as they say." He indicated the other woman in the room. "You remember Ms. Sanchez, I trust?"

Elizabeth nodded to the social worker. "How do you do?"

"I'm fine. Nice to see you again."

"There will be time for pleasantries later," Judge Bursey interrupted. "I mentioned earlier that we would need a home study completed. I have here a preliminary report from Dr. Mayberry stating her initial findings, and one from your son's neurologist, Dr. Muller." He peeked over the top of his glasses at Elizabeth. "By the way, I'm pleased to hear that his seizures are settling down."

"Yes, they are, thank you."

"Good, good. Dr. Mayberry has several concerns."

Elizabeth frowned. "But he's doing better. She even said so. He's using some words now and..."

"Be that as it may, the psychologist notes a number of troubling areas. As you mentioned, his language development is an issue, although I'm glad to hear that you note some progress." There was a note of skepticism in his voice.

"Dr. Mayberry does not seem to feel that it is anywhere near where it should be for his age."

"I agree, but he was set back by our experiences. And he's recently started seeing a speech/language pathologist who is pleased with how he's coming along."

"I see no mention of that in Dr. Mayberry's report."

"She knows. She said she would include it."

"Possibly it's coming in her next report." He put down his papers and folded his hands. "Court begins next Monday. Have you made childcare provisions for your son? My secretary is unable to add that responsibility to her other duties."

Now, that was unfair, thought Elizabeth. Before she voiced her thoughts, Ms. Sanchez jumped in.

"Your Honor, Ms. Whitmore has arranged appointments with my office for myself or some of my staff to be in the playroom with Timothy during court time next week. On two of those days, I will be with him, as part of the assessment you ordered."

Elizabeth looked at her, torn between gratitude and questioning just what this woman would be assessing.

"I'm glad that is taken care of. Now to some other areas Dr. Mayberry addressed." He perched his glasses on his nose and skimmed the pages in front of him. "There are some questions about the level of isolation being inflicted on the child. She feels that he would benefit from interactions with more people than just his mother. It says something about lack of stimulation hindering brain development."

"What! I provide my son with plenty of stimulation."

"Such as sitting him in front of a screen the way he is right now?" Judge Bursey indicated his outer office.

"No! That's something fairly new. He's only been interested in Paw Patrol since he's gotten to know the neighbor's dog."

"Oh, that's a good show for kids," added Anna Sanchez. "You mentioned a dog?"

"Yes, our neighbor has a little Bichon named Blitz that Timothy enjoys playing with. The dog and the neighbor's little girl. She's a little older than Timothy, but they seem to get along well."

"How often do they get together?" the Judge wanted to know.

"A few times a week, sometimes more when Cynthia, the mom, babysits him."

"Good. Glad to hear that you're not making a hermit out of the boy. He needs to be with other children."

That wasn't fair. They'd huddled together after the ordeal of being kidnapped and being betrayed by Timothy's father. Who wouldn't?

"He's four. Have you enrolled him in school for the fall?"

"No, not yet. I feel like I've just had time to catch my breath after what we went through. And this trial stuff is taking up a lot of time and energy. Plus, we have a lot of appointments to attend." Need she remind the Judge that most of these extra appointments came about because of *him*?

Judge Bursey shuffled the papers, straightened the edges, and placed them in a file folder. "I'll leave the two of you to coordinate your calendars to arrange for the next home visits. Initially, one planned and one surprise visit per week, and then the rest at Ms. Sanchez's discretion." He stood. "You are dismissed. Please give my secretary a copy of the schedule you work out." He left the room.

Chapter Eighteen

"Well, that was, ah, pleasant." Elizabeth's upbringing wouldn't let her be openly critical of someone like a judge.

"A little overbearing, do you think?"

"That's one way of putting it."

"I know that Judge Bursey can come across a bit heavy-handed; it goes with the job. But I've worked with him for a number of years now and know that he has the best interests of the child at heart."

"I'll take your word for it. It doesn't feel like he has *my* best interests at heart, and my interests and those of my son are intertwined."

"Yes, they are." She pulled out her day planner. "You need to look at this from his point of view. He's used to trying custody disputes."

"Custody," interrupted Elizabeth. "There's no question about custody here. His father cannot look after him from prison. Plus, if you'll remember, that man tried to have his son's mother killed!"

"Alleged." She returned Elizabeth's stare. "During

court, crimes are 'alleged' until they make a conviction. That's just the way our legal system is.

"Judge Bursey has seen more things than you can imagine when it comes to the welfare of children. He has a soft spot for kids and has grandchildren of his own that he dotes on. Believe me, his staff hears more about those kids than they ever wished."

"Why does he have it in against me?"

"He doesn't, truly, he's just concerned. He didn't like that your son accompanied you to court each day when the trial began. Apart from hearing things not meant for a young boy's ears, sitting on a wooden bench for hours at a time is not natural for a child of this age. The fact that Timothy was so quiet alerted the judge to the fact that something might be wrong."

"There *is* something wrong. He was kidnapped by a nutcase. His father arranged a separate kidnapping and murder for me. He's a child with a seizure disorder who was without his crucial medications. Yes, those are all wrong things." Her chin jutted out. "And not one of them was my fault."

"Yes, you were clearly a victim in this. We don't want to see you victimized any more, nor do we want Timothy to pay further for what you both went through."

"Then why do I feel like I'm being victimized all over again with the Judge prying into our personal lives?"

"I'm sorry. I see how you could feel that way. He's not against you, really, and neither am I. Our priority is the well-being of your son. Since his father is now out of the picture as far as parenting goes, and the Judge questions some of the choices you made in bringing Timothy into the courtroom, it is not unusual in these circumstances to request a psychological consult and home study."

"These 'circumstances'. I'm not a fan of many of the circumstances we've been through recently."

"I understand. Really, I do, and I see that you love your son. Sometimes when horrendous things happen to us, we need a little help and that's okay." Anna had been through this before. "I know that you can't see me as a friend, but try to think of me as someone trying to help." She pulled out a pen. "Now, can we talk about dates?"

She used to think that she knew how to parent - didn't give it a second thought, just acted on instinct. The only parts that threw her were the medical aspects of the seizure disorder, but she'd gotten a handle on that. She *thought* she was a good mom – maybe better than good. That is, until Judge Bursey got on her case.

She shuddered to think how her mother would have reacted to learning that Elizabeth was at odds with someone in authority. Appalled, for sure. That just wasn't done.

There was a time when she would not have given her decision a second thought, but now her life was full of second-guesses. She knew that routine was important in a child's life. Timothy's bedtime had always been seven-thirty. They never deviated, well, except while they were kidnapped, and even then, she had tried to make their existence resemble as much of their home life as possible.

But tonight was different. It was seven-thirty and dark outside. Yet, here she was, holding tightly to Timothy's hand as they strolled the street.

She never should have listened to Cynthia. Sure, her neighbor meant well, but she didn't know Timothy and how stressors could affect his health.

She held tight to her son's hand. They'd stay just a few minutes, then get back to their routine.

Almost never had Timothy been out at this time of

night. She looked at her son. At least he didn't seem tired, and there were no dark shadows under his eyes. Instead, he looked intrigued by all that was going on around them. They strolled, taking in the sights and the sounds and the people. The tension left her shoulders. They'd be safe here, amid these people who at least knew each other by sight and knew who belonged here.

Their quiet street was transformed today. Neighbors formed committees and work bees to create a block party. Not sure she'd even heard of them before, Elizabeth was cautious. But the activities seemed family-friendly and Timothy was by far not the youngest child out here.

Lawn chairs lined every yard. Many driveways were filled with homemade booths and activities. They stopped to watch a puppet show. The costumes were rough and the stage crude, but to the children watching, it was magical. The slapstick antics of the puppets drew enthusiastic roars of laughter from the audience.

At another yard, a series of plastic pop bottles were half-filled with sand. Kids (and adults) were invited to try to throw rubber sealer rings over them. Anyone successful got a popcorn ball. Elizabeth steered Timothy away from that one. She could just imagine what the carbohydrate load of one sweet popcorn ball would be, considering the starch from the corn and the gooey caramel coating that held it together.

Timothy almost toppled over with the force of a body leaping on him from behind. His mother's firm hold on his hand held him upright. Rather than frightened, Timothy turned around, curious, only to be engulfed in a hug from his friend, Amy. Behind (farther behind than Elizabeth thought appropriate for this time of night), Cynthia waved to them, admonishing her daughter to not be so rough.

"Isn't this great?" Cynthia's enthusiasm matched that of her daughter. "So glad you came."

Elizabeth felt a tug on her arm, then Timothy's hand fell away from hers. She reached for him, but Cynthia said, "It's all right. I know where they're going. Come on." She linked her arm with Elizabeth's and followed the children to two houses up. "Amy's done this already but wants to try again."

Set up in the Smith's yard was a toss game. A slanted board had round cut-outs, with numbers painted under them. Kids lined up for their turn to throw bean bags into the holes. It didn't seem like anyone was keeping score; after taking three throws, each child got a mini chocolate bar.

Amy put hers in her back pocket. Timothy inspected his, but when Amy said, "Come on!", his got shoved into a pocket as well. Good. Maybe Elizabeth could rescue it and throw it in the garbage before he had time to wonder what it was. Timothy had never had a chocolate bar in his life. Messy things and too high in carbs for a ketogenic diet.

Amy pulled him along. It's not that Timothy was a reluctant participant, but his head was too busy swivelling this way and that, taking in the colored lights, music and activity that had overtaken their quiet street.

Elizabeth worried about her son getting overexcited. If that happened, he'd never get to sleep. A good sleep was preventative as far as seizures go. But a bit of a late night just this once couldn't hurt, could it?

Across town, Dr. Mayberry joined her mentor, Dr. Arnold Murphy, at a restaurant.

"I heard that you lost a patient." Arnold's statement had a question behind it. "Was he a long-term client?"

"Yes, I'd been seeing him for almost four years."

"Tough."

"Not so much. He'd been clinically depressed for years. Meds didn't seem to have much of an impact, but then, he never took them consistently."

"He didn't understand how they worked?"

"Partly. But it was more than that. He actively resisted the fact that he needed them, didn't want to depend on chemicals to make him function. And his depression would affect his cognition, his sense of time and, you know…".

The food arrived, and they tucked in.

Hanna thought about that patient. He was one of her annoying ones, with intractable depression that never seemed to lift much. Cognitive behavior therapy only worked so far with him.

It was trying, listening to him whine week in and week out, year after year. He wouldn't take his meds consistently. He wouldn't persist through initial sideeffects to see if a different medication would help him. There was always a trade-off; you couldn't put artificial chemicals into your system without expecting the body to react in some ways, both positive and negative. Sometimes you had to suck it up and tolerate some unpleasantness to eventually become more functioning.

But Bill wasn't into it, would not tolerate any discomfort, like a dry mouth, or weight gain. So, he had to put up with major discomfort of a long-term depression. For years he'd talked about suicide, that it just wasn't worth the effort anymore.

She'd helped him to think about that rationally, picture what his life was like now, how it had been for the past few years and what he had to look forward to in the future. It was the future that got to him, decades more of semi-existence. He made a choice to consume all the medications he'd stored up for the past few years, guzzling them with bourbon. She didn't agree with his choice of beverage, finding the brand he chose to be harsh, but that was up to him. As far as she was concerned, he made the right choice in the end. They were both now out of his misery.

But Arnold didn't need to know all of that. He had his own intractable patients.

Later that night, she stood alone at the patio window. Past the blackness outside, distant lights reflected off the water, just past her expanse of manicured lawn.

This was a place built for children. She could picture a swing set and play box over to the left. A fort would be perfect under sheltering branches of that weeping willow.

Yes, this was a place meant for children. One child in particular. Soon, Dr. Mayberry promised herself. Soon.

Chapter Nineteen

Elizabeth rose from Dr. Mayberry's sofa. She used two hands to push herself up, rising like a woman of twice her age and three times her weight. Did she stagger a little on those first few steps? Get hold of yourself. She could hear her mother's words in her head. A lady does not emote all over the place.

She plastered a smile on her face for Timothy. Her son did not need to see how affected his mother was by Dr. Mayberry's words. She reminded herself that this was all for Timothy's sake - everything was.

"Hello, little man." Dr. Mayberry, her voice cheerful, as if she hadn't just nuked Elizabeth's hard-won composure.

The psychologist ruffled Timothy's hair, pleased when he didn't pull away from her. He was becoming more and more accepting of her presence, of her touch. Good. "Can you say, hi Hanna?"

"Hi."

It was better than nothing, which is what she would have gotten from him at the start of their sessions. He'd never said 'Hanna' yet, and certainly not 'Dr. Mayberry', but that the latter was to be expected. 'Hanna' would come, she was sure of it.

This time she led him to the dollhouse. She had several models but had brought out the one most closely resembling the home where he lived. She wanted to learn more about his life there and his interactions with his parents. Well, his mother, really; his father was a thing of the past. Too bad the man hadn't realized what a treasure he had in this little boy. Or maybe it was better for her that he hadn't. After all, without this trauma, he might never have crossed her door. Now, *that* would have been a tragedy.

Rather than have Timothy take the lead in the play today, she had some specific purposes in mind, so guided him in the directions she wanted to pursue. First, they started in the living room. Dr. Mayberry set out a child, a man, and a woman doll. "Show me playing in the living room."

After a few moments' hesitation, Timothy picked up the child and sat it on the living room floor.

"Who else is there, playing with the little boy?"

Silence and no actions to include an adult. Dr. Mayberry made some notes. This child was left to play on his own. His mother's past made her hold back, depriving this precious little boy of the sort of interactions crucial to his development.

"Where's the mommy?"

Pleased that his receptive language was strong enough to follow her directions, Dr. Mayberry took notes. Timothy placed the mommy in the kitchen. Sometimes he moved her to the den, down the hall from the living room where Timothy played. This would interest Judge Bursey.

As Timothy's interest waned, Dr. Mayberry reminded

herself that he was just four, and a four-year-old who was mainly left to his own devices. She knew what he would like now, something relaxing to prepare him for the next part of their session.

She lifted Timothy onto the sofa, his legs dangling. "Just wait a second. I'll be right back with a surprise." She opened the narrow door on the other side of the room, bent down and scooped up Honey. She brought her over, laying her gently in Timothy's arms. His eyes sparkled as his arms carefully embraced the cat, then he began stroking her silky fur. Her purr filled the room; Timothy's face filled with wonder.

Good. This was the right time to introduce the next part of her plan.

She brought over the headphones and set them on Timothy's head. He no longer shied away from them, having gotten used to wearing the headphones during part of their sessions and listening to the music, both here in therapy and at home. From how comfortably he was wearing them, she didn't doubt that his mother meticulously followed her directions to use them several hours a day. Sometimes having a client who was a rule-follower was a good thing. It helped a plan come together.

Using the remote control, she started the tape she had spent so many hours compiling. It began with the Gregorian music Timothy was used to. She could tell when her voice kicked in by his startled glance in her direction. To begin with, her voice was soft and encouraging, saying soothing, sometimes nonsensical things. Then the sounds switched to Mozart and Timothy settled back, intent on the purring creature on his lap. Dr. Mayberry pretended to work at her notes, watching Timothy from the corner of her eye.

She again knew when the tape switched by the telltale

signs the child gave off. Change was hard for him, she knew. That's why the tapes switched things up, she told his mother. Change was a fact of life for all of us; he needed to learn how to deal with it. What better way than from the safety of her office and from his own home?

Timothy's eyes widened at the words coming through the headphones. Yes, another sign that his receptive language was intact. He stopped petting the cat; Honey butted his hand to get him to continue again. Good old Honey - she really was a helpful therapy cat.

Timothy resumed, but the petting was more mechanical now. Although Honey liked it, Timothy's former enjoyment seemed to have vanished. Well, he'd get used to it. Auditory Integration Therapy took time. Dr. Mayberry smiled.

The next morning, they went to Dr. Mayberry's office. She wanted to see Elizabeth first. "I'd like to revisit some of what we talked about previously, about the time when your brother drowned."

Elizabeth's brow furrowed. "Do we have to?" Some things were better left alone. She had not enjoyed the feelings that session dredged up.

"Yes, we do. Without adequately examining some of our prior experiences and how we dealt with them, our unconscious mind can color our present actions and beliefs with these unresolved issues."

"I don't think things are unresolved. My brother died. He died saving me and I couldn't help him." More quietly, "I didn't help him."

"Exactly."

"Pardon me?"

"Let's talk about that." She crossed her legs and angled

her shoulder toward Elizabeth. "Did your parents blame you for the accident?"

"No! You just said it, it was an accident, a drowning accident."

"But if it were not for you, that riptide would not have swept away your brother. Is that correct?"

Very quietly, "Yes."

"I'm sorry. I didn't catch that."

Louder, "Yes. If it weren't for me, he would not have been in that area."

Sitting back, Dr. Mayberry changed tactics. "Were you your parents' favorite?"

"No, I don't think so. They loved us both equally."

"Did they? As a parent, it is hard to love each child equally. Some personalities just fit, some traits are shared, and the bond is closer. Was it that way in your family?"

"They doted on my brother. Oh, they loved me too, definitely, but he was the first-born. Their hopes for carrying on the family line and the family business rested on his shoulders. It wasn't said in so many words, but the expectation was there." She lifted her eyes to Dr. Mayberry's. "He was a neat guy. Strong and smart, not afraid of anything. He was interested in so many things and excelled at whatever he tried. He was a good big brother, always looking out for me." Her voice quavered. "Obviously. And he died doing just that."

"Do you ever regret that day?"

"All the time. At first, every waking minute I regretted it. I regretted that I didn't stick closer to the shore. I regretted that I didn't keep swimming closer to Jonathan. Why couldn't I have paid more attention? And I regret that he saw me.

"It would have been better if I had been the one swept out to sea. That would have been easier on my parents."

"How so?"

"My parents were so sad."

"And they wouldn't have been sad to have lost you?"

"Of course, they would have. But it would have been different. They pinned so many of their hopes on Jonathan. They slated him to take over the company, follow in our father's footsteps."

"Could you not have done that?"

Elizabeth looked shocked. "No, that was not a possibility. It was not even discussed."

"Why?"

"Well, the business world is tough. It's competitive and requires someone with a robust constitution."

"That doesn't describe you?"

Elizabeth shook her head. "No, definitely not. Daddy called me his delicate flower, his little lady." Then she grew wistful. "Sometimes, when I was really young, I felt like I could do all sorts of things. But it wasn't encouraged in my family. Girls were to be looked after and cherished."

"Did your parents cherish you?"

"Definitely. Even more so after Jonathan was gone. It was like they had to protect me after they'd failed to protect their son."

"Did they protect you?"

"Yes. It was like they were opposed to taking any chances. Going away to college was a big deal. They wanted me to get an education but didn't want me to leave the protection of their home. If I had stayed living with them, the only school close by was a community college and they didn't want that for me. They settled on Vassar. I mean, *we* settled on it. They wanted me in Bryn Mawr and

I almost went there, but I wanted to take interior design and Vassar had an affiliation with The New York School of Interior Design. If that's the field I wanted, they preferred that I go to the best, so we decided on Vassar.

"They picked the sorority I joined." At Dr. Mayberry's raised eyebrow, she explained, "I was just a kid of nineteen. What did I know? They'd both earned degrees and had a better sense of what would be suitable for me."

"I see."

The silence lagged, but Elizabeth didn't know how to fill it.

"Do you think your parents were relieved to have you out of the house?"

Puzzled, Elizabeth said, "No, I don't think so. Why would they?"

"Would you have been a constant reminder of the child that they lost?"

Elizabeth's head jerked up like a marionette's, controlled by someone off-scene.

Dr. Mayberry continued. "You're a parent now. You know how you feel about your child, your first-born. Do you think your parents blamed you for their only son's death?" She looked at her watch and rose. "Our time's up now. Would you change places with Timothy, please?"

Chapter Twenty

Anna waited while Elizabeth undid the three locks. She reached for the screen door without realizing that that one, too, needed to be unlocked. "Thanks for having me in your home."

Elizabeth's grin belied her words. "Well, it's not like I a had a lot of choice." She held out her hand. "I know that this wasn't your idea."

"In all honesty, while this is the Judge's order, I don't think it's a bad idea."

Elizabeth raised her eyebrows.

"For all of your sakes - yours, your son's and the Judge's."

"We'll see. Come on in." She led the way to the living room where Timothy lay on his stomach, carefully putting pieces of Duplo building blocks together. "He just woke up from his nap," she said, explaining his distinct case of bedhead. She tried smoothing his hair back into place.

"I visited a mom the other day who bemoaned the fact that she can no longer get her four-year-old to nap. Instead, he gets overtired and whiny by supper time and she struggles to get the food on the table. It must please you he'll still nap."

"It does, but I know it won't last forever." She brushed his hair some more. "There's a definite difference on those days when we have appointments in the afternoon, and he misses his nap. We try to stick to a routine as much as possible, but lately, it's been hard."

"It must be tough juggling all that you have to do. How many appointments are you going to?"

"He has regular appointments with his pediatric neurologist, although we may move to monthly if he continues on the path he's on right now. Depending on the results from the neurologist, we might need to see the pharmacist for a medication tweak. That happens more often than you'd think. Things are getting better though, seizure-wise. We're seeing the psychologist, Dr. Mayberry, weekly. He now has weekly speech/language pathology appointments. Then, as you know, when court is in session, we're there for at least half-days; he's either in your playroom or with our next-door neighbor during court appearances." She paused. "It seems like a lot."

"It *is* a lot, more than most young mothers have to contend with. And, on top of all that you've been through."

Elizabeth sat back, relaxing somewhat. Maybe this woman got it. "Would you like more tea?"

"Yes, but could we go into another room to talk? Is your son all right in here alone a few minutes?"

"Of course. If we go into the kitchen, we can see him from there."

As they settled at the kitchen table, Anna said, "Look. There are a few things that I'm required to do. Could we get them out of the way before we have a chat?"

"Certainly."

Anna got up from the table and opened the fridge door. At Elizabeth's expression, she explained that she had to confirm that there was food in the house. At Elizabeth's insulted expression, she said, "There are certain boxes I have to tick. I know that to you these are basics, the essentials, but you never know…Now, would you please show me your son's room? Then we can relax and have a visit."

While Timothy's bedroom was not in pristine condition, it looked like a place where a wee boy lived and played. A single bed, with Thomas the Tank Engine sheets and comforter, a bookshelf, two toy chests, and kid-sized desk and easel completed the furniture. Most of the toys were stowed away in their bins, but not all.

Anna walked to the bookshelf and pulled out *Where the Wild Things Are*. "One of my favorites."

Back in the kitchen, they cradled cups of tea. Away from the courthouse, Anna seemed less an extension of Judge Bursey's hand, although Elizabeth kept foremost in her mind that Anna would report to him.

"How are the sessions with the psychologist going?"

"For me or for Timothy?"

"Both."

"Well, I don't have to fight Timothy to go to see her, so that's a good sign. She has a cat which he adores."

"Pet therapy is quite effective with some people."

"Seeing how Timothy reacts to that cat and how he loves playing with our neighbor's dog makes me wonder if we should have a pet."

"What's stopping you?"

"Allergies. We don't know for sure what my son might

react to, but stressing his immune system with allergens could make his seizures worse. He had a rough time when he was off his meds when we were, ah, taken…" She took a sip of her tea before starting again. "But now that he's back on them regularly, with a few prescription changes from Dr. Muller, he seems stabilized. I'd hate to rock the boat, but he seems to love these animals – both the therapy cat and the neighbor's dog. I plan to talk to Dr. Muller about it at our next appointment."

"That's a tough decision. I hope your doctor gives a pet the okay, but," she looked around the pristine home, "having an animal in the house is a big adjustment."

Elizabeth laughed. "Big adjustments are what we're all about these days, it seems."

"No kidding. Not least of all is single parenting. How are you finding it?"

"That part is not much different. I've always been the stay-at-home parent, so I have done most of the caregiving. Jackson's job took him away from home often, so it was just Timothy and me for most of the week." She refilled each of their teacups. "And even when he was here, our roles pretty much determined that I handled Timothy. Jackson was uncomfortable with the physical and medical aspects of Timothy's care."

"How are your sessions with Dr. Mayberry?"

Elizabeth sighed. "If we're talking about comfort, they're not my most favorite part of the week."

"But you're going?"

"Haven't missed an appointment and don't plan to." She leaned forward and whispered, "I'm scared of Judge Bursey."

Anna's grin lit up her face. "He's not so bad once you get to know him." At Elizabeth's looks, she added, "Truly.

He means well, but it is all pretty austere with the robes and chambers and all."

"Tell me about it. You should see it from my side of the desk."

"What's an appointment with Dr. Mayberry like?"

"Scary." She covered her mouth. "I shouldn't have said that."

Anna encouraged her with a nod.

"I mean, she's not actually scary, but you never know which topic she'll bring up and she doesn't mince words."

"She must think that you can handle it."

Ruefully, Elizabeth admitted, "I'm not always sure I can."

"Therapy can be tough."

"You're not kidding. She wants to delve into things that happened twenty years ago."

"Like what?"

Elizabeth sighed. "I suppose you'll see it in some report, anyway." Bolstering herself with more tea, she said, "When I was nine, my brother died. He died saving me, and a riptide swept him out of sea. That changed a lot for me and my parents."

"I'm so sorry your family went through something so horrific."

"Dr. Mayberry wanted to delve into my feelings about that day. It wasn't pretty."

"Sometimes we have to confront old wounds in order to heal from them and move forward."

"Yeah, I get that. Truly I do, although it hurts."

"Those sayings about time healing grief? I'm not always sure they're true."

"I miss my brother and I'd give anything to have changed the events of that day. But I can't and I've learned to live with that." She laced her fingers together but didn't notice her leg dancing up and down. "Dr. Mayberry asked me if my parents blamed me for his death."

———————

The bell rang. Had Anna forgotten something when she left?

The monitor showed Jake standing at her front door. Another man stood behind him, surveying the street. Goodness. They used to go weeks with no one ringing their doorbell and now twice in one afternoon.

She couldn't pretend they weren't home, not with Jake, who had been nothing but kind to them. Although she was not a fan of males these days, these two were the exception.

"Hey, Elizabeth. How are ya? We were in the area, so we thought we'd stop by to see how you're doing." He indicated his partner. "You remember Brendan James, my partner?"

How could she forget? "Of course. How could I forget the man who saved our lives?"

"No, ma'am. You saved yourself and your son. I arrived just in time to clean up the mess and haul away the trash." He shook her hand, holding it in two of his own and giving a gentle squeeze. "How have you been?"

"Better than the last time you saw us, that's for sure." Although she'd prefer that this conversation would end here, and she could wave the men on their way, courtesy demanded more. "Would you like to come in?"

Elizabeth and Jake nursed their coffee at the kitchen table. Not far away, Brendan was on the floor, pushing toy trucks around with Timothy. The man seemed to have an infinite repertoire of vehicle noises he could make. Impressed, Timothy tried imitating some.

"Although I want him to talk more, those are not quite the utterances I had in mind," said Elizabeth. She didn't mean it critically; her joking skills must be rusty.

Brendan scrambled to his feet, giving the hair on Timothy's head a gentle ruffle. "Sorry. I got carried away. Didn't mean to teach the kid any bad habits." Why was he so nervous around this woman, Brendan wondered? It made it hard to do anything right.

"I'm kidding," Elizabeth explained. What was wrong with her that she even had to explain her comment? She shouldn't be sarcastic with this man to whom they owed so much.

As they were leaving, Brendan had one last question. "Would you mind if I dropped by again some time?"

Chapter Twenty-One

"And then do you know what he said?"

Dr. Mayberry brought her gaze back to Mrs. Schroeder, a long-time client. Really, she should have dismissed this woman years ago, but patients like this made up her bread and butter. They showed up faithfully week after week, month after month, year after year. How many years had it been now? Going on for half a decade. And what had changed? Nothing. Well, apart from the rates that Hanna charged. If she was going to sit through the same old, same old every single week, she deserved to be well-compensated for it. Mrs. Schroeder's husband, the same one she was whining about right now, could afford it. Hanna wondered if the man happily forked over her fees so that *he* didn't have to listen to his wife's harangues.

Enough. There was only so much she could take, despite this woman's fees keeping her in good wine. She interrupted. "You've been married for quite some time now. Is that correct?"

"Seventeen years," replied Mrs. Schroeder.

"Do you ever feel like the excitement has gone out of your marriage?"

"Yes!" She went on to explain ad nauseam the ways that her husband ignored her and didn't appreciate her.

"Have you considered that it might not be entirely your husband's fault?"

Bella Schroeder hesitated. "*I* haven't changed. *He's* the one who's become so wrapped up in his job and his reputation."

Dr. Mayberry appeared to consider this. "I wonder if there is something that you can do to liven up your marriage, bring back some of that spice, the anticipation of surprise that you had when you were first getting to know one another?"

"I, I don't know. I can't think of anything. I already dress nicely and make good meals."

"Sometimes a man needs more than that, especially after the same old, same old for so many years." She appeared to think. "I once had a client who tried something."

Bella leaned forward in her chair.

Continuing, Dr. Mayberry chose her words carefully. "I'm not saying that this would work for everyone, or even that it was the right move for her, but..." she tried to look uncomfortable, "she began doing the housework in the nude."

At Bella's gasp, she elaborated. "With the drapes open."

"Oh, my god!" Though shocked, something in Bella's eyes sparkled.

"Her husband came home unexpectedly one day and found his wife like that, bent over, cleaning the oven."

"What happened then?"

Dr. Mayberry just raised her eyebrows.

As they had several times now, Keira and Daniel dropped by. Sometimes she called ahead; sometimes they just stopped in.

Elizabeth was unused to drop-ins. Getting together with friends had always been planned and agreed on ahead of time. This spontaneity threw her at first, but Keira's exuberance won her over. Plus, Timothy so obviously enjoyed playing with Daniel. For two mostly nonverbal little boys, they seemed to communicate with each other.

Today, the two women shared a bench, watching their sons play in the sandbox at the park. Timothy's formerly pristine Tonka trucks now showed signs of scratches and dents since they'd been used outside. The boys dug and loaded trucks and dumped them. Neither Keira nor Elizabeth could figure out the game, but the boys seemed in sync with it.

"Maybe we could ask Jake to build you a sandbox in your backyard. Daniel loves the one he made for him."

"I'd have to check with the gardeners, but yes, that might be nice." She wasn't sure where it would go in the manicured yard, but maybe there was a spot.

Keira's face scrunched. "Whose yard is it anyway? Why would you need to ask anyone to do something on your own property?"

"It's a courtesy, really. The gardeners have been in charge of the landscaping since we moved in and I've never interfered. Sort of a sign of respect to their workmanship, you know?"

No, Keira didn't know. She said "My house, my rules."

Elizabeth smiled. Maybe that wasn't a bad philosophy.

"How's it going with the shrink?" asked Keira. "I'm not sure I'd like someone poking around in my head."

"She's a psychologist, not a psychiatrist. And it's going.

She's helping Timothy; he's saying a few words now. I can't predict when they'll come out, and it's not consistent, but it's a start."

"Daniel's speech is the same way."

That gave Elizabeth pause. "He's also now seeing a speech/language pathologist."

"Ah, now that's something I could get behind. The one at Daniel's school has been really helpful - not so much in making him talk, but in helping him communicate. She's helped him understand and follow routines and rules." Her eyes met Elizabeth's. "They lost him once; he ran off from the playground. Scariest hour of my life. But that's not the only time it happened - he got away from me while shopping and he left our house a couple times without me knowing. Hasn't happened since we got the visuals and rules in place."

Elizabeth could not imagine losing Timothy. How would you even start looking for a small child who doesn't answer to his name?

"Dr. Mayberry might be gentle with Timothy, but she's brutal with me. Or at least that's how it feels." It wasn't like Elizabeth to share personal information, but something about this setting—the sun, the air, the laughter of their sons, lowered her normal guard.

"How could that be helpful?" It made little sense to Keira.

"She seems to think that I'm 'closed off' and that that might be due to past trauma."

"Well, you are a bit uptight, but I thought that was just you."

Elizabeth returned Keira's grin. From someone else, she might have been affronted, but Keira was so honest and warm, it was hard to take offense. They were an unusual pair. Keira sat slouched on the bench in torn jeans, a worn denim jacket, and red sneakers minus their laces. A thin strip of Elizabeth's skinny jeans was visible between her knee-high black leather dress boots and her belted London Fog trench coat. While Keira's spiked pixie-cut hair pointed up, Elizabeth's smooth, low ponytail flowed down her back.

Elizabeth hesitated. Other than her parents, she was not used to confiding in anyone. What did that say about her marriage?

Her parents had been gone for almost five years now, and even when they were alive, some subjects just seemed taboo. Once, when she was a young teenager, she had tried to talk to her mother about her brother's death. "Better to let the past stay in the past," had been her mother's way of shushing her.

"Maybe my mother's way was right," she told Keira, "because dredging it up sure hurts."

"I'm generally a fan of pushing unpleasant memories away. On the other hand, I always used to push people away, too."

"Me, too."

"I had trust issues."

"Me, too." For two women seemingly so different, they had much in common.

"Jake changed that for me. Boy, did he push," laughed Keira. "That guy couldn't take a hint, and I was as blunt as I could be."

Elizabeth did not doubt that. "What changed that?"

"He wore me down. Little by little, I let him in. Actually, Daniel let him in first."

Curious, Elizabeth asked, "Do you regret it?"

"It was scary to begin with, but no, I don't regret it. Not at all. He's been the best thing to come into my life since

Daniel." Her eyes grew soft. "I've gone from thinking that all men are crap to believing that only some of them are crap."

"Progress, I guess."

Back at the house, Elizabeth, Keira, Timothy, and Daniel sat around the kitchen table, chasing miniature marshmallows in their cups of cocoa, when the doorbell rang. The camera showed Cynthia.

Opening the door, Elizabeth started to ask, "Are you alone?" Amy barrelled by her, followed by Blitz. She answered her own question. "No, you didn't come alone."

Amy skidding past the kitchen, noticed Timothy and slid back in. "What are you drinking?" Then, "Who's this?"

Keira introduced herself and Daniel. Cynthia prodded Amy to shake hands politely. The three kids took off to play in the living room with a promise that they'd be called when more hot chocolate was ready.

"Sorry to barge in like this," began Cynthia. "We only meant to stop by with an invitation. It's Amy's birthday on the 8th and we're having a small party for her. Would you and Timothy be able to come? She specifically asked for Timothy." She turned to Keira. "It sounds like the three of them are getting along."

They all listened. Only Amy's words were distinguishable, although the boys made sounds and there was movement and laughing.

"Would you and Daniel like to come as well, please? We'd love to have you."

Elizabeth excused herself to answer the phone.

"Hello, Ms. Whitmore. This is Ethan Bauer from Jackson's office. I'm sorry to bother you at home, but we were wondering if we could drop by and pick up your husband's files. We've reassigned his clients and cases but are missing some key files. He travelled and worked from home a lot; we're assuming that the files we can't locate are in his home office."

"I'm sorry, but there are no files here. The police emptied Jackson's office and took everything with them."

"I see." Silence. "Ms. Whitmore, I feel that I should warn you. There are some, ah, irregularities in the files we've been going over. Funds unaccounted for. Unusual methods of detailing assets and expenses. Would you be able to give me the name of the detective who has the files?"

Chapter Twenty-Two

It had become their habit that Elizabeth put the headphones on Timothy after his nap, while he played on the floor. But the past week, he'd begun jerking his head away when she tried to put them on him. She examined the padded earpieces to see if anything poked him. No, they looked fine. She placed them to her own ear and pressed play on the remote. No, the volume was at a comfortable level and the music came through nicely.

"Timothy, Dr. Mayberry wants you to listen to this."

He held still long enough for his mom to position them, then start the recording. Once Elizabeth returned to the kitchen, he shoved them off.

Entering Cynthia's home was like stepping into a different dimension. Generally, their house was reasonably staid, apart from Amy's exuberance. Still, things were orderly and calm. But today…

Timothy froze. This was not the Blythe home he knew.

Behind him, Daniel stopped, not sure if he should flee or just remain on high alert. Keira placed both of her hands on her son's shoulders and pushed down firmly, grounding him.

Amy came running by, grabbing the boys' hands, and pulling them into the living room. Elizabeth had her doubts that they would go with her, but they followed.

"Well, I guess we're here," remarked Keira.

"Her house is not usually like this," explained Elizabeth.

Cynthia beckoned them into the kitchen. "Hi, thanks for coming. Would you believe that there's only ten kids here?"

No, they wouldn't.

Cynthia set them to work making sandwiches and cutting them into small triangles. Next, they spread a sheet on the family room floor to serve as a tablecloth, arranging paper plates and cups, then the platters of sandwiches, cups of juice and slices of raw vegetables.

Then Cynthia called for their help in the other room. They directed the kids in a line to take their blindfolded turn at pin the tail on the donkey. It surprised Elizabeth how well the kids waited their turn. Keira explained that these kids looked to be about five so would all be in school. A big part of school seemed to involve lining up, so they were used to it.

"Is Timothy enrolled in Pre-K?" Cynthia asked.

Good lord, thought Elizabeth. Just one more thing to think about. But there wasn't time to dwell on that problem. Cynthia needed their help in arranging the next game. They split the teams of two into lines of four. The first child in line minced forward, cradling a balloon between his knees, to pass it off to the next child on his team, amid cheering and leaping and howling. Elizabeth was not sure that all the kids understood the rules of the game, but they were enthusiastic if their yelling was an indication.

Watching Timothy, Elizabeth knew that she had to alter her thinking. She'd been sure that this was an environment far out of her son's comfort zone. He would *not* enjoy either the commotion or rubbing shoulders with this many kids, especially kids he didn't know.

But, instead of being a quivering mass on the sidelines, Timothy was right in there. While not a leader, he followed others and didn't shy away from their games. Although how he could figure out the rules was beyond Elizabeth. To the children, it didn't seem to matter. What was important, apparently, was noise and motion. Yes, they had plenty of both.

Timothy's face wasn't one of being overwhelmed; rather, it held delight.

Elizabeth thought of all the times she had carefully shepherded him away from contact with other kids, leaving the playground when others arrived, trying to keep her son safe from the roughhousing she witnessed other kids engaging in. While she knew that her son wasn't exactly breakable, his seizure disorder and likely allergies did put him at risk for assaults on his immune system, which could trigger more seizures.

Yet, in working so hard to protect his physical being, had she deprived him of opportunities to develop in other ways? Just because *she* didn't feel the need of a social life, did she have the right to deny Timothy one?

Before the excitement got too out of hand, Cynthia called a halt, shepherding the children into a line, then into the other room to eat. It was semi-orderly. It tempted Elizabeth to herd the kids toward the bathroom to wash their hands before eating, but she didn't voice her concern. No one would have paid her any attention, anyway.

Astounding how many sandwiches these little people could consume and in short order. After asking Elizabeth to bring out the plates and forks, Cynthia entered, balancing the birthday cake and lit candles on her outstretched arms. Kneeling carefully, she placed the cake in front of Amy, with directions to make a wish, then blow out the candles.

Elizabeth tried not to cringe as Amy blew all over the cake, spittle contributing to the dousing of the candles. When she had trouble with two of them, friends on either side of her willingly leaned over to lend their breath and saliva to the task.

A rousing rendition of Happy Birthday came next.

As she and Keira helped cut, serve, and pass around slices of cake, she momentarily forgot about Timothy's keto-genic diet. He'd already eaten his share of sandwiches. He was halfway through his portion of cake, apart from what he wore on his face. He ate with delight, as if this were an entire food group new to him.

Most of the kids finished eating. Some backed around the sheet, others ran overtop of it as they raced back to the other room. Cynthia's hope that the food would settle the children down seemed futile. Where there was a momentary lessening of the noise level, the kids seemed to push through that quickly, and get back to their boisterous enjoyment of the party.

Cynthia sat on her heels, regarding the mess on the floor. Keira brought in a garbage bag and began gathering up the paper plates and cups. Cynthia's energy flagged; the kids' energy levels escalated.

The screaming in the other room took on a different tone, then Amy shrieked for her mother.

The women ran into the other room to see a circle of children regarding a flailing child on the floor.

Timothy! A tonic-clonic seizure shook his small body. The smell of urine filled the air.

"Eww, he peed!" yelled one helpful child. The others watched, some frozen, some horrified. One little girl cried; another joined in.

"Move back, move back," instructed Keira. "Give him room."

Elizabeth pushed her way through the frozen bodies to kneel beside her seizing son. His limbs had a life of their own, pulled by strings controlled by the misfiring in his brain. The muscles in his neck and arms corded, the tension in his little body tough to witness. Saliva pooled at the side of his mouth and ran down to the floor. As his arms and legs thrashed, his head moved to a rhythm of its own. Elizabeth slipped her hands under the back of his head, cradling it from further abuse on the hardwood floor. She studied her son, fighting her panic and horror to watch objectively. Dr. Muller would want a report. Yes, although his movements were all over, the jerking was stronger on the right side and his head consistently moved toward his right shoulder. Likely the seizure originated from the left side of Timothy's cerebrum. She feared that this might set back his newly developing language skills.

Keira ushered the other children back into the other room, saying, "Who wants more cake?" That did the trick, although some looked back at their friend on the floor, fear in their eyes.

As Timothy's tremors slowed, Elizabeth turned her son onto his side, in the recovery position. Resting a hand on his forehead, she spoke softly to him, her reassuring tone meaning more than the words. When the final tremors left

Timothy's body, and he slumped, Elizabeth gathered him to her.

Not only had he wet himself, but his bowels had let loose as well. This was not uncommon with such seizures, but he'd not had any for a while. Rising carefully, Elizabeth cradled Timothy in her arms.

Keira was there to hold open the door for her. Clutching Daniel's hand, she followed them to Elizabeth's house. As she held that door open for Elizabeth, a car door slammed.

"Hi, Elizabeth," called social worker Anna Sanchez. "I hope this isn't a bad time for a home visit."

Elizabeth froze, then staring straight ahead, continued into her house. She sat in the padded rocking chair and gathered Timothy closely in her arms, the same chair where they had spent countless hours together when he was a baby.

In the hallway, hushed voices whispered.

"What happened?" asked Anna.

"He had a seizure."

"The poor child. I thought they were better."

"So, did I. So did Elizabeth." Keira peeped around the corner to see how they were doing. "Timothy seems asleep."

"That's common after a seizure. Apparently, they're exhausting."

"Not only for the kid, but his poor mother," Keira added. "You should have seen Elizabeth. She knew just the right things to do. I'd have frozen or become a screaming maniac if that had been my child."

"Somehow, I don't see Elizabeth as a screaming maniac type. And she's been with him when he's had seizures before. But I had the sense she thought that these were over."

Keira whispered into the living room. "Is there anything I can do?"

Automatically, Elizabeth shook her head. Then her manners kicked in. "No, thank you. He's sleeping now. I'll just sit here with him for a few minutes, then I need to get him cleaned up."

Anna's head appeared beside Keira's. "I'll go get a bath ready for him."

When Elizabeth stripped off her son's soiled clothing, Anna snagged them from the floor and put them in the washing machine. It felt like the least she could do.

Keira settled an exhausted Daniel on the couch for a nap and then made tea. Although her preference was to cuddle up with her son and catch some rest, she sat with Anna at the kitchen table.

"You look like you've been through the ringer, as well," observed Anna.

"No kidding!" Keira ran a hand through her spiky hair. "Of course, nothing like what Elizabeth's going through." She blew out her lips. "Have you ever been to a birthday party with five-year-olds?"

"No, can't say that I have, thank goodness. But I can imagine."

"Well, ramp up your imagination mega times and there you have it." She stretched out her back. "Cynthia said there were only ten kids in her house. She swore it was true, but I don't think she can count. How could she when those rug rats never held still in one spot long enough for us to blink?"

"Was it fun?"

"Who are you asking? Me? Well, maybe in some

perverse way. It was nice to see the kids so excited and enjoying each other's company. If you're asking about my son and Elizabeth's, yeah, the boys had a good time. Although Daniel's in Pre-K, and so mixes with other kids, whenever I've been in his classroom, it's orderly and not frenetic. Today, was well, it wasn't like that. Sort of like a free-for-all, but our sons were right in there - racing around and doing goodness knows what, but grinning." She brushed her forehead with her arm. "I guess that's the important part."

"What happened to Timothy?"

"I should let Elizabeth tell you that part because I have only a rough idea. He had a seizure and I think it came on quickly. One minute he was happy and fine, and the next, he was on the floor." She sipped her tea. "Elizabeth knew what to do for him. Even though it felt like it went on forever, it probably only lasted a few minutes."

"Less than that," said Elizabeth from the doorway. She looked haggard. "Is there more tea?"

Keira fetched a cup and a saucer for her.

After taking two fortifying sips, Elizabeth turned to Anna. "I must apologize. This was not the kind of visit you expected. Now you've seen us at our worst."

"What I saw was a concerned mother caring for her ill child. I admire how calm and in control you seemed - exactly what Timothy needed."

"What he needed was to not have another seizure." Elizabeth's retort came out more sharply than she'd intended. "Sorry. My nerves are still on edge. I'd thought, I'd hoped that we were past this." She pushed her hair behind her ears. "Maybe we'll never be over it."

"Whether or not his seizures subside, you'll be there for him and you'll handle it."

Elizabeth blinked. "How can you say that? You hardly know me."

"I know what I saw today," Anna said. "And I know what I observed the last time I was here, and I know from the trial records so far and neurologist's report that you've done an admirable job of mothering that young boy."

"That's not the impression Judge Bursey gives, not at all."

Chapter Twenty-Three

"How many more sessions do you think this will take?" Elizabeth led with a question as soon as she entered Dr. Mayberry's office. In her head, Elizabeth's mother frowned at her. She would not be pleased at omitting the pleasantries before getting into the meat of the visit. But Elizabeth needed to know.

"Why, dear? Are you worried about the bill?"

"No, I can afford it. It's just that it takes a lot of our time when there is so much going on in our lives."

"Might it be worth it if resolving these issues now allows you to live your lives more fully later on? Is this something you owe to Timothy?"

Well, when she put it like that…?

"How is the trial going?" asked Dr. Mayberry.

"It's going. I don't really have anything to compare it to."

"Must be hard to sit there and listen to evidence of your husband's perfidy."

"Yes. Yes, it is." No one could know just how hard it

was. The one thing she was grateful for was that mother and daddy never had to know the extent of the betrayal from a man they'd accepted into their family.

"Why do you think he did it?"

"Excuse me?"

"Why do you think he tried to eliminate you from his life?"

The question seemed too personal. But, she reminded herself, that's why she was here. Her mother's admonition of 'keep yourself to yourself' didn't apply in a therapy room. "Money, I guess. At least that's what's coming out in court."

"Did you not give him an adequate allowance?"

Elizabeth frowned. "Allowance? I didn't give Jackson any allowance."

"Ah."

What was that supposed to mean? "Jackson had his own money. We each had our own money. He worked; he had a good job. Money was not a problem."

"And yet, he tried to have you killed so he could access your money."

"Allegedly." That's what the defence lawyers kept saying. Innocent until proven guilty.

"But you know, don't you dear?"

Yes, in her heart, she knew.

Dr. Mayberry continued. "And you didn't see any of this coming? Didn't sense that something was intrinsically wrong at the heart of your marriage?"

Staring at her hands as she folded and unfolded them, Elizabeth gave a small, "No." Maybe if Daddy had been alive, he would have clued in on the problem earlier and prevented this whole mess. He'd always taken care of her.

"How do you think it could be that something so fundamental as love and hate in a marriage could have passed you by?"

Elizabeth flinched. Then some of her father's genes showed themselves. "You don't pull any punches, do you? Isn't that rather blunt?"

"Trying to deflect the question? That's not something you should try with me. I've been doing therapy for years. With some clients, it is necessary to cut to the core, especially after years of erecting walls around themselves.

"But we'll take a different tack, if that will help." She sat back, her expression serene. "Tell me about this 'daddy' you talk about. What kind of man was he? A parental figure often points clues to the spouse that we later seek."

"My father was a wonderful man. He devoted his life to taking care of us, my mother and me." Elizabeth warmed to her topic; this was comfortable ground. "Nothing flapped him, he was always calm and in control. I never heard him utter a harsh word to us. He was always loving and handled everything. We didn't have to worry about a thing."

"How did that change when you married Jackson?"

"It didn't, not really. Though, of course, it was now up to Jackson to smooth our way."

"Was he up to the task?"

"Certainly. It wasn't that hard; daddy made sure of that." She shifted her body, angling towards the psychologist. "As a wedding present, he bought us our house. He called it our 'starter home', as it is quite a bit smaller than the one where I grew up. But it has four bedrooms, plenty of room for the two of us, then the three of us. And it's in a good area; daddy made sure of that."

"How did Jackson feel about such a substantial wedding gift?"

"He was pleased. Why wouldn't he be?"

"Hmmm."

"That meant that none of Jackson's salary had to go towards anything like a mortgage. Daddy also arranged a house fund for me, like a trust fund, but used for household expenses. And, when he learned that I was expecting Timothy, he bought me a new car. My previous one was just two years old, but Daddy felt that a larger Mercedes Benz would be safer for a child. Quieter, too, he said, with a better air filtration system. He wanted only the best for his grandson." The grandson he never got to meet.

"What was the house fund used for?"

"A yard service, utilities, any repairs that came up, groceries, gas, you know, usual stuff. Daddy wanted us to have a housekeeper, but we didn't need one. With just the two of us and Jackson away so often for work, the place didn't get that messy. Two days a month a woman came in to do deep cleaning and I kept up with the rest."

"And this woman was…."

She had hoped to avoid this part. "Barbara. The woman who came to clean was Barbara."

"The same Barbara…".

"Yes. My husband's girlfriend." Then she added, "Ex-husband. But at the time, I didn't know about their involvement."

"Should you have known?"

"I would have liked to have known. Maybe there were clues, but I didn't see them.

"When she came over, Timothy and I would go out. You know, to leave her free to get on with things without us being underfoot. And the smell of the cleansers bothered Timothy; he'd have breathing problems. We needed to be careful with things like that in case they precipitated a seizure."

"So, you left this woman in your house alone with your husband."

"Only sometimes. Often Jackson would be away at work." She thought about it. "But it seemed like he was spending more and more time working from home, in his office." Yes, his work-from-home days often coincided with the days the cleaner was scheduled to be there.

"And you had no clue?"

"Sometimes not as much got done while we were away as I would have expected. But you never know; some of these cleaning aspects aren't obvious unless you're really poking around. Although, the last time, I wondered. At supper I mentioned to Jackson that I thought Barbara was to wash the insides of the kitchen cupboards that day, but it didn't appear to get done. He said something about hearing her rattling around in here but didn't pay attention to what she was working at." That was also the day Elizabeth had come home to find their bed rumpled and the sheets untucked. She distinctly remembered making the bed as soon as she got up in the morning. It was a ritual she never skipped, smoothing the sheets, tucking them taut, and pulling the bedspread just so. It was nice to get into a pristine-looking bed at night. It looked like someone cared.

There were other things, little things. Like she and Timothy would come home to find some of their furniture rearranged. Jackson said that the maid probably didn't put it back correctly after she vacuumed. Other things were out of place. Elizabeth wasn't so anal that every item needed to be in its proper place, but over time, she'd gotten used to certain things being in certain places and it looked odd, them being out of place. And once, an unusual scent lingered on her favorite bathrobe, a scent that didn't match any of her shampoos, soaps, or perfumes. Now these little things added up, but at the time it didn't cross her mind that the maid would take liberties with Elizabeth's things or that her husband was taking liberties with the house cleaner.

"Let's get back to your husband."

"Ex-husband," reminded Elizabeth.

"Yes, the soon-to-be ex-husband. What do you think could drive a man to such desperate actions?"

"From what is coming out at the trial, money seems to be behind his actions."

"Yet, he had a good job. If your father took care of your basic living expenses, what did Jackson spend his money on?"

"Clothes. He loved to dress well. Even though we divided the walk-in closet in half, his suits spilled over into my side. Eventually, he moved a lot of his things into one of the guest rooms."

"A person can only buy so many clothes. What else did he do with his money?"

"He enjoys sports cars. He leases them and changes cars every two years. He'd be pumped with one for maybe the first six months and then dream of his next purchase."

"Did that bother you?"

"Not really. We all have our passions."

Dr. Mayberry regarded Elizabeth steadily. "And what are yours?"

Not the question she expected. Timothy came to mind. "My son, of course."

"You say, 'my son', rather than 'our son'."

"Timothy used to be our son. Now, he's just mine."

"Apart from having a son together, what attracted Jackson to you?"

"Oh, I don't know. What attracts one person to another?"

"Let's back up. What do you think attracted your parents to one another?"

"That's easy. Elegance. They were both classy people. Mother was gentle and everything a lady should be. Daddy was strong and enjoyed looking after us. Mother basked in his care and devotion. Daddy loved the soothing home she created for us. She was also supportive in his business, hosting parties and solidifying contacts he needed."

"Did you provide those same things for your husband?"

"To a lesser extent. Jackson didn't require the same social connections for his work. But I created a welcoming home and a relaxing life for him."

"How did he and your father get along?"

"Fine. He and daddy golfed together. We had dinner at their place every Sunday. They didn't talk daily the way I did with my parents, but they were close."

"Why do you think your husband wanted to have you killed?"

Elizabeth left Dr. Mayberry's office feeling pummelled. The psychologist must think she was a tough nut to crack, so she had to be harsh. She kept reminding herself that she was going through this for her son's sake; for Timothy, anything was worth it.

She was pleased that Dr. Mayberry always seemed so gentle with Timothy. She must adjust her therapy approaches to what she felt each client required to make progress. So, was leaving each session exhausted and depressed progress?

Thankfully, Timothy never looked the way Elizabeth felt when he left the psychologist's office. And, other than the first couple of times when it was all new to him, he didn't show reluctance. Although, the last time, he seemed different, more on edge when they left. Maybe it was a forewarning of an upcoming seizure. He dragged his feet today, but that could still be the aftermath of this week's seizure.

Oh, that reminded her. She turned back to Dr. Mayberry's inner office. "Before Timothy comes in, I forgot to tell you one thing. It may be nothing, but this week, Timothy was reluctant to wear the headphones. Prior to this, he didn't fuss at all when I put them on him, but he didn't seem to like them these last few days."

"Might have something to do with an unsettledness prior to his tonic-clonic seizure. Without a constant EEG, it's hard to know what sort of electrical storms are going on in his little brain." She rose and made a shooing motion with her hand. "May I ask you to leave now and send Timothy in? You're taking up some of his time and after all, he's the primary concern here, isn't he?"

Chapter Twenty-Four

It was evening, after hours, and they were old friends. Although Dr. Arnold Murphy was her therapist, their relationship was complex. Friends, yes. Therapist-client, not quite. It might have started out that way, but over the past two decades had morphed into more. A comfortable, platonic more, where Hanna felt that she did not need to put on a facade as she did for her patients.

Like many of those conscientious people in their field, both Hanna and Arnold had mentors, counselors they met with from time to time.

Theirs was a field fraught with peril. Carer burn-out was an occupational hazard. Listening to people's grief all day, whether of their own making or imposed on them by others or circumstances, took a toll. Not getting sucked into the miasma of depression took a stable, grounded person, especially if the psychologist strove to be of help to their clients, while maintaining their own mental health.

Checking in periodically with an esteemed colleague

was prudent, both for the psychologist and the clients he or she served.

They each sipped a glass of wine - a nice merlot Hanna had brought along.

"Any interesting cases?" He asked, knowing that Hanna would respect her client's confidentiality and mention no names or details that could lead to him knowing their identities.

"Maybe a few twists to old ones. There was that annoying, whiny woman who shows up religiously to lament her husband and how boring her life is. I swear, I could repeat her stories word for word." She grinned. "In my head, of course." She cradled the bowl of her wine glass in both hands. "Although I shouldn't say she is always boring. This week she threw in a new twist." This time her smile was devilish. "You'd never believe it of this plain-Jane, prissy, middle-aged woman, but she is now doing housework in the nude. And she's hoping for a deliveryman to ring the doorbell."

"From what you've said before, this sounds out of character for her." Concerned, Dr. Murphy asked, "Has something happened?"

"I think that eternal boredom got the best of her and she ran with an idea."

"Is she safe?"

"Oh, yes. She's too mousy to do anything more than prance around her home by herself in her birthday suit."

"Hmm. This one bears watching. She could be heading for a breakdown."

Although conversation between the two of them usually flowed easily, tonight their silences lengthened. Hanna stared off into the reflections on the darkened windowpanes.

Watching her, Murph asked, "Is something on your mind?"

"Oh, just the usual. You know. Listening to the minutiae of people's lives all day can get a bit wearying."

"That's why we strive to keep a balance in our personal lives."

"Huh! What personal life?"

That was not like Hanna. "Are you displeased with your personal life? Has something happened?"

"More like nothing has happened." She sat back, waved a hand, and gave a half-smile. "Oh, ignore me; I'm fine. It's just that I've felt my biological clock ticking more this last while. I had expected to be settled with a family by this age."

"You can still make that happen; you're not that old."

"I know."

"You're a beautiful woman, smart and accomplished. If it's a relationship you're seeking, there are plenty of men out there who'd love to be with you."

"Thanks for saying that, Murph. You're a good friend."

"It's not like you not to take action when you feel a void."

"You're right. I go after what I want." She smiled, a warm one this time.

"How are things going with that little boy you talked about?"

Hanna's eyes took on a sheen of excitement. "Great! He's coming along well in our sessions. We've really connected."

"Is that your goal?"

"He needs to if we're going to make any progress. His

mother has kept him so isolated that he doesn't know how to relate to other people." She warmed to her subject. "That mother." She shook her head. "She doesn't deserve a child like this. He's sweet and has so much potential, but she has hindered his development. And last week, she put him at risk. He had a grand mal."

"What would she have done to induce that?"

"She went from keeping him totally isolated to exposing him to a rambunctious children's birthday party, full of screaming, strange kids."

"Weren't you complaining that she kept her son too isolated?"

"Well, yes, but moderation is important. She should have worked up to a gathering like that. It was too much for the child."

"Hmmm." To him, it sounded like a typical experience for a kid of that age.

"She's lucky the seizure didn't set him back. We won't know for a while though."

"Is much coming out in therapy?"

"Some, but it's slow. We've mainly been working on trust so far. He's comfortable with me now, and he loves Honey.

"He's been responding to the Auditory Integration Therapy." She stopped when she noticed the look on Arnold's face. "I know, I know, you're not a fan. But I use what works for each individual. It's helping Timmy. He's speaking more and is open to new experiences now."

"Just because two things occur around the same time, does not mean that one caused the other. Correlation does not imply causation," Arnold reminded her. He noted that she used the child's name - something they never did when discussing patients.

"Oh, I know, I know. But my gut tells me it's working,

and our profession is as much art as it is science." She sipped her wine. "Last week I notched the recordings up another step, adding affirmations into the music."

"What affirmations?"

"Just the usual, what you'd expect a four-year-old to hear and internalize." She smiled into her wine.

Chapter Twenty-Five

Saturday morning. Elizabeth lingered over her coffee. No appointments, no commitments today. It had been quite a week. She relished the time to just relax and get back into their comfortable routine, just the two of them.

The doorbell rang. Elizabeth pondered how she might disable the darned thing. Was it too much to ask for a quiet day?

Checking the monitor, she spied Keira's spiky hair. Was that *blue* glinting in the sun? She shook her head. Whoever thought that she'd have a friend with *blue* hair?

She opened the door and Daniel barrelled in, his head swivelling in search of Timothy. "He's playing in his room. Go on up." There was no need for her to add that last bit, as Daniel was already halfway up the stairs.

"Just wait until they can yell for one another," laughed Keira as she gave Elizabeth a hug.

Behind her pushed in Jake, a cocky glint in his eye as he

slung an arm across Elizabeth's shoulders and squeezed. A more sedate Brendan waited his turn, with a hug. "Hi," he said. "I hope it's okay that we dropped in."

"Oh, of course it is," said Keira. "Otherwise, we wouldn't be here." Her confidence never failed to surprise Elizabeth. Nor her bossiness, it seemed, as Keira added, "Get your coat on and grab Timothy's. We're heading out."

Frowning, Elizabeth asked, "Where?"

"A picnic, of course. What else would you do on a gorgeous Saturday?"

Elizabeth could think of a thing or two. Actually, many multiples of twos.

Daniel came barrelling back down the stairs, Timothy on his heels. They breezed past the adults, out the front door, and wrestled with the handle on the unfamiliar van that parked in Elizabeth's driveway.

"Hey!" Elizabeth yelled after her son. He never went to strange cars. Ever.

Brendan backed out the door and pressed the button on his key fob, unlocking the van's door. "That's my van, or rather a rental I picked up for today."

At Elizabeth's questioning look, he explained, "We couldn't figure out how to get the four of us plus two kids with child seats into any of our cars, so I picked up this van." His face reddened. "We were hoping that you'd come along."

Jake said, "Wanna throw me your car keys and we can transfer Timothy's car seat into the van?" When she made no move to do anything other than process what was going on, Jake spied her keys in the pottery dish on the side table near the door and scooped them up. "Great. It'll just take me a second, then we'll be ready."

"But…"

"Nope, no buts allowed today. It's decided. Grab your coat."

With that, Keira left, following the men, settling the kids into the back seat of the van.

Elizabeth had no choice but to follow. They had her son.

They hiked. Elizabeth had not realized just how much sitting she'd been doing lately. She needed to get back in shape. Weight was never something she'd worried about; she ate sensibly, and neither seemed to gain nor shed pounds. But, watching Keira and the men's easy strides, while she tried not to pant to keep up, was a reminder to make some changes.

Changes. That seemed to be all her life was about these days.

Her eyes followed the little boys. Now, *they* certainly had no trouble with this walk. In fact, they probably covered three times the miles as they ran circles around the adults, on and off the path, stopping to inspect something, and then racing ahead.

This was a change for the good. She'd never seen Timothy like this - earlier this week, racing around with the kids at Amy's birthday party, now out playing with Daniel. Thoughts of the birthday and the seizure brought a frown to her face. She'd better watch that he didn't get overexcited in case...

A hand on her arm stopped her worrying. "He's all right," said Brendan. "Look." He pointed. "He's happy and having a great time in the fresh air with his friend. What could be wrong with that?"

Elizabeth's smile was rueful. One shoulder shrugged. "Yes, you're right. It's just hard. If you've never seen a seizure, you don't know how scary they can be. And the possibility of brain damage is always present, especially if they get out of control again."

"I have witnessed seizures. In my line of work, you do. Those were with strangers; I can only imagine what it's like if it's your own child."

"Do you have kids?" Elizabeth asked.

"Nah, never had any." He hesitated, then added, "Not married, either. I was once when I was eighteen. My girlfriend got pregnant, so we got married. Seemed like the right thing to do at the time, but she lost the baby. She lost interest in me, too, shortly after, so we parted. We were just kids."

"I'm not married either. Sort of, or soon I won't be. But I guess you know all about that."

"Yes. I met your ex."

Elizabeth rolled her eyes.

They both thought about the scene at the hotel where Russell Rose Allen held her and Timothy captive. The door had flown open, revealing Jackson standing there with a gun. Relieved and believing him there to save them, she'd been so shocked when his bullet slammed into her shoulder, that the pain didn't register. His second bullet struck Russell Rose's chest, and he collapsed on top of Elizabeth. Jackson had then snatched Timothy from the bed, fled the room and passed the child to his girlfriend. Elizabeth could still hear Barbara's words in her head, "Ewww. He's pissed himself."

Jackson yelled at her, "He's a child. He's had a seizure. Take him!" Then he stepped back into the hotel room, his gun pointing at Elizabeth. Before he'd taken three steps, Jackson and Barbara had been surrounded by Brendan and Jake's team, ambulance sirens in the distance coming closer.

The trail steepened and rocks made the footing uneven. Worried about her son, Elizabeth looked for Timothy. He and Daniel were already past that part and running into the meadow, following Jake.

Brendan took her hand to help her over this section of the path. She started at his touch, then relaxed. Once they were on level ground again, he let go, careful not to overstep with Elizabeth. Spooking her would be all too easy. He'd like to see where this could go with Elizabeth, but knew that she was not ready. So, he'd wait.

He didn't want their day overshadowed with horrific memories of what they'd been through. Since she'd brought up her ex, maybe they should talk about that elephant, get it out of the way.

"I've seen you at the trial," he began.

"Who would have thought it would take up so much time?"

"Ah, I would," answered Brendan. "Part of the occupational hazard when you're a cop." But, to him it was a job. To her, this was her life. "Must be pretty tough to listen to." If she wanted to talk about it, he'd give her an opening.

It was easier to talk about while walking. She could keep her eyes on the ground. "No kidding. Even though right after it all went down, I learned that it wasn't just Russell Rose after me, but other people as well. And, despite the hints that these other kidnappers were hired by my husband, it didn't really sink in until I heard their testimonies in court." She walked on a bit farther. "To think that my own husband, the man I lived with for seven years, hated me so much that he wanted me killed."

Brendan couldn't help himself. He gave her hand a squeeze but held on this time. "That's a reflection on *him*, not you."

She gave a half-smile. "Thanks, but not totally true. What does it say about me that I didn't even know that my husband detested me that much?"

"From what I understand, it might not have been hatred for you, but greed on his part. He wanted easy access to more money and saw you as standing in his way. Plus, his girlfriend goaded him."

"There's that, too. How could I not have known that my husband was unfaithful?"

"I think that happens to too many spouses. It did to me, and I hadn't seen it coming."

It was Elizabeth's turn to squeeze his hand.

The sound of stomping little feet heralded the imminent arrival of Timothy and Daniel. Elizabeth quickly pulled her hand from Brendan's.

"Mommy!" Timothy was there, yanking on her other hand. "Eat, eat!"

Words! Proper words, the sort that anyone could understand. Elizabeth's heart soared. She'd feared that this last seizure might have set his development back. But he'd said words today, more than one, and appropriate ones.

"Food?" questioned Brendan. "Let's go!" He hiked a little boy under each arm and ran on ahead, the kids' squeals of delight wafting back to Elizabeth. Brendan looked back over his shoulder to check that Elizabeth was coming.

"I did a thing," said Keira. They all sat on the blanket and Keira opened a box of crackers, then a container of dip. "I bought this yesterday." She held up the dip for their inspection. "It's avocado hummus dip. I like avocados. I like guacamole made from avocados. I like humus. What could go wrong? I took a taste last night and my mouth said, 'No! Just no!'" She handed the cracker box to Brendan. "Here, what do you think?"

"I like hummus and I like guacamole," he said as he loaded his cracker up with the greenish spread. Opening wide, he chewed. Then stopped. His eyes widened and his brow furrowed.

Jake laughed at his friend while Keira waited for him to try it. "Brendan is a wuss about any new foods. He makes us go to the same old restaurants all the time. *I* have much more cosmopolitan tastes." He dug into the dip with relish. His grin remained in place for the first chomp. It slipped a bit with the third, but then he searched frantically for a napkin to spit into.

Keira had one ready. "See?" She turned to Elizabeth. "Liz? Want to try?"

"It's Elizabeth and yes, I'll try some." It was a standing joke between them. Keira tried to get away with calling her Liz, but Elizabeth was having none of it. Keira tried calling Timothy Timmy once, but Elizabeth was clear that that was off limits. There was only so far Keira wanted to push their friendship, but she could not resist needling Liz.

Elizabeth was always encouraging Timothy to try new foods; if he had his way, he'd stick to the same few meals he preferred. "Just one bite," she'd tell him. How could she do less now? Besides, she was a fan of both hummus and avocados. But, after watching the men's reactions, she bit cautiously. Her eyes widened as the flavour combination assaulted her taste buds. Good gracious! How could two such excellent foods blend together so badly? Keira was right - no, just no.

"Guess that's unanimous, then." Keira set both aside. "Good thing we brought plenty of other food."

As the four of them arranged the feast on the blanket, no one at first noticed Timothy. He sat on a corner of the blanket with his legs crossed. On one knee perched the opened container of avocado/hummus dip. He'd pulled the plastic bag of crackers from its box and was happily munching away, taking a cracker, generously dipping it into the green humus, then repeating his actions.

Keira handed the empty cracker box to Elizabeth. "Here. They're almond crackers, gluten-free. I know you're watching Timothy's diet, but you can check the ingredients yourself. The hummus is organic and contains just avocado, chickpeas, garlic, and olive oil. I think you can trust it."

Chapter Twenty-Six

"I wonder if it's the waffling that is getting to you, Mr. Bronx." She had had it with these depressed, weak males who couldn't make a decision if their life depended on it. She snickered, hiding her face behind a tissue, and pretended to sneeze. That former patient, the one who OD'd on pills, finally did make a decision, a major one. The next question pulled her out of her reverie.

"What do you mean, Dr. Mayberry?"

"How long have you been coming to see me?"

"I don't know. More than a year, anyway."

"I checked before you came in. We have had eighty-two sessions together. How much progress do you feel you have made?"

"Not much. I'm not feeling any better, maybe worse some days."

"Exactly my point. After all this time, don't you feel that you should have progressed?"

"But when we started, you said there was no timeline,

that the person was an individual, made up of his past and his choices."

"True, and I'm pleased that you remembered. Do you recall what I also said?"

"That we don't have control over our pasts, but we have control over our choices."

Dr. Mayberry nodded - a teacher pleased with a star pupil. "Which brings us back to the waffling I mentioned."

Bronx's blank expression showed that he wasn't following.

Inwardly rolling her eyes, Dr. Mayberry leaned forward. "You came to me complaining of depression, a depression not relieved by the medications prescribed by your family physician."

He nodded. "And they made me feel funny."

"So, we changed those meds." She glanced at her notes. "Several times, in fact." She gave him a penetrating stare. "Your compliance wasn't better with any of them."

Bronx squirmed. "They made me feel funny. And the depression didn't go away."

"Of course, it didn't. Mood disorders don't disappear on their own. Medications give us a chemical edge to help patients move in the right directions, but easing those lows takes some cognitive effort on our part." She waited a beat. "Doesn't it, Mr. Bronx?"

"Yes, you've said that before." A pleading tone entered his voice. "I tried; really, I've tried, but my life doesn't get any better." He crossed and uncrossed his fingers, staring at his hands.

"Let's talk some more about that waffling. Sometimes indecision is harder than deciding. Waffling can get us caught in a loop, with thoughts going around and around in circles, weighing each endless possibility, until it's worn out.

That can create an inordinate amount of stress on the mind and the body, wearing down all your systems."

"Worn out. That's how I feel. When I came to you, it was because of my thoughts of ending it all. My doctor referred me here because he thought I was suicidal."

"And were you?"

"Yeah, I was. I mean, I am."

"Passive people can have a tough time in life. They feel that everything is done to them, without them having any agency over their own lives. We've talked before about making strides towards taking control. How has that been working?"

"I've tried, but no matter what I do, things just don't get better. They still ride me at work. My bank account hovers around the same balance, barely making it through to the next pay check. I can't get ahead. I come home exhausted and my apartment looks like a hovel, but I don't have the energy to clean up."

"What's going to change?"

"Nothing." The bleakness in his eyes should have haunted Dr. Mayberry, but they didn't. Briefly she wondered why, but she could think about that later.

"Looks like you have some decisions to make. Are you finally ready to take action?"

"Are you sure you're okay with keeping him today?"

"Definitely," said Cynthia. "I just hope that you feel okay trusting him in my care. Again, I'm so sorry that he had a seizure during Amy's party."

"Not your fault. Most likely it would have happened, anyway. It's hard to predict when they might occur. It had been a while, and I'd let my guard down, maybe missed some signs. I'm sorry that the kids had to witness it; it can be scary, even when you've seen them many times before."

"Poor lad. I'm sad that he has to go through this, that both of you do."

Elizabeth settled in front of Judge Bursey's desk. Why did this make her feel like a rowdy kid, sent to the principal's office?

"I have two reports here, one from Ms. Sanchez based on her home visits and one from your psychologist, Dr. Mayberry." He looked over his glasses as Elizabeth. "I must say that the two paint quite different pictures."

"I can explain," began Elizabeth. "Anna's surprise visit came at a bad time." She blushed. "I suppose you hear that all the time, but this truly was a bad time. Timothy had just had a seizure, a tonic-clonic one, and he was only semi-conscious when she got there. It had been a while since he had one like this; Dr. Muller felt that medications had it under control…"

The Judge interrupted her. "I understand. Ms. Sanchez's report is quite favorable about how you handled that emergency, and on your son's progress in general."

"Oh." Well, that was nice. She hadn't thought Anna would go against her, but you never knew if people were the same to your face as they were behind you back. Plus, she didn't know exactly what Anna would look for.

But wait. The Judge had said that the two reports differed.

"Your psychologist seems to have many more concerns. Since she was your choice, we need to give what she says some weight."

"What does she say? Can I see it?"

"At some point, you'll have access to the documents. For now, they are the property of the courts. But I can give you some highlights. Here are some of her concerns:

- the degree of isolation Timothy suffers at your hands
- inconsistencies in your parenting, going from keeping him only to yourself, to exposing him to a boisterous birthday party in a house teeming with small, overexcited children
- his major seizure is a worry and Dr. Mayberry questions if it might have been brought on by medications administered in a haphazard fashion
- allowing the child to be humiliated in front of his peers when he wet and soiled himself at that same party
- part of her treatment plan is Auditory Integration Therapy, but she notes that you admit to not using them at home in the way she has prescribed"

With each point the judge read out, Elizabeth went from shocked to enraged. This was unfair and just wrong. Things were taken out of context. How could Dr. Mayberry say such things?

Judge Bursey continued. "Dr. Mayberry also talks about her sessions with you. Adequate parenting is necessary for Timothy's development. She mentions your lack of insight into your own life, not realizing the extent of your husband's animosity. To be fair, she mentioned that there are two sides to every story. Although she is aware of your husband's alleged crimes, she states that so far in therapy, she has been unable to get to your contributions to the situation. Your son's isolation at home with only you has interfered with his development, both socially and language-wise. She talks about you being closed off, and emotionally unavailable to your son." He paused and regarded Elizabeth. "I appreciate that these things must be difficult to hear."

Difficult? She was speechless. How could she combat this?

"Don't worry. She has some solutions and recommendations.

"She feels that your son requires more intensive therapy than can be offered with once-a-week sessions, or even multi-appointments in a week. It is key that he develops relationships with other people. Since he has bonded with her, she has made a very generous offer. She recommends that Timothy spend time with her consistently. She is willing to suspend appointments with her other patients for a week, and devote herself only to Timothy during that time, at her home, twenty-four hours a day.

"She explains that this will be the most relaxed setting for him and that with just the two of them, his bond with her will build, priming him for other, positive relationships later in his life."

Horror filled Elizabeth's heart and face. She had never, ever been away from her son, not for more than a few hours at a time. "Can she do this? Can she take my child?"

"Now, Ms. Whitmore. Don't look at it that way. No one is 'taking' your child away from you. It is our policy to keep families intact whenever possible. Sometimes there needs to be a brief separation until things are in place in the best interests of the child."

"But…".

"My ruling is to comply with the esteemed psychologist's recommendations. You will deliver the minor child, Timothy, to Dr. Mayberry's office at one o'clock on the afternoon of November 15th, along with a week's supply of clothing."

"But that's in three days!"

"Yes. With a child this young, and has experienced his level of trauma, we need to proceed expeditiously."

"May I contest this? Get a lawyer?"

"It is always your right to obtain counsel. But my ruling holds. Three days, Ms. Whitmore." He rose. "Dismissed."

Anna waited in the hall for Elizabeth. Elizabeth staggered and momentarily looked at Anna without recognition. Anna said her name and squeezed her arm, partly for emotional support, partly to hold her up. "I see that you received the news."

Elizabeth's voice returned. "How can she *do* that? How could she *say* those things about me? And how could the judge believe them?" She turned to Anna. "How could he take Dr. Mayberry's word against yours?"

"I'm sorry, so sorry. I submitted my report first and wrote it as honestly as I could. If I'd known what Dr. Mayberry planned to put in hers, I might have worded parts of mine differently. But I didn't see this coming. In all my years doing this, I've never heard of a psychologist offering to take a child into her home like this."

"But he's *my* child. Mine! I have custody. How can they take this out of my hands?"

"The court has the right to take over care of a child when it deems it is in the best interest of the child."

"How do I fight it?"

Anna regarded her kindly. "I don't think that you can. I

know that this is not what you want to hear, but I think that the best thing you can do is to comply, then it will be all over, and Timothy will be back home with you."

Elizabeth stiffened, her upbringing coming to bear. She backed away from this woman whom she had thought was on her side, who understood her and her son. "Thank you for your time. I take it that our involvement is over. You've submitted your report, and this is the result."

"But…"

Elizabeth kept walking. She left the building alone. She had let down her guard, let people in, even just a bit, trusted and look what happened. She placed her hands on the top of her steering wheel, then rested her forehead there.

Murph raised his eyebrows as Hanna signalled the server for a second glass of wine. His own was still almost untouched. They'd only sat down less than ten minutes ago.

Interpreting his questioning gaze, Hanna said, "It's been a tough week."

"And…". His chin pointed to the now refilled wine glass.

"Definitely one of those with ups and downs." She composed her face into what she knew Murph would understand. "I lost a patient this week."

They both knew what she meant by "lost." But just to be sure, he asked, "Lost?"

She nodded. "Suicide, yes. Hung himself."

"Was this a sudden change in status?"

"Not really. He was a sad little man who had struggled with depression for decades."

"Had you been seeing him for long?"

"Almost two years." She shook her head. "We made

little progress, although lately, I sensed that he was trying to take more control of his life." She gave a half-smile. "I guess he did."

"Sometimes ours is a tough profession." He waited until her gaze met his. "How are you holding up?"

She shrugged. "You know how it is. It's hard not to take it personally."

"We are not in control of our patients' lives; we can only offer guidance. The choices are up to them."

"I know, I know all that head stuff. But sometimes my heart just wants to take over for them, especially when I know what's best."

Murph watched his protégée as her wine glass was topped up again.

Chapter Twenty-Seven

She had no recollection of driving home. Pain and loss and helplessness surrounded her.

How could her life have gone so wrong? She'd been a good girl, never giving her parents a moment of grief. She didn't rock the boat, ever, and followed all the rules.

So how could stuff like this happen to her?

She stopped the car but didn't get out. How could she face Timothy now? How could she tell him? She needed a few moments to get herself together.

Shutting her car door as quietly as she could, she glanced at the house next door. Could she get inside without Cynthia realizing she was home and wondering why she didn't immediately come for Timothy? Her habit was to go directly from the car to Cynthia's door. They'd share a cup of coffee, and a chat while the boys finished up their game before she and her son headed for their home. But today, Elizabeth could face no one. Not yet.

She curled up in the recliner and rocked. How many times had she held Timothy in this very spot, lulling him to sleep, cradling him after a seizure or just enjoying the closeness? Would she ever do that again?

Why wasn't daddy here when she needed him most? He never let her down. He'd know what to do. He'd never have let any of this happen to her in the first place.

But he wasn't here, and she was on her own. Own. All by herself. That fact was never clearer than today.

She rocked and mourned. She had lost it all, lost everything. Her brother was gone. Her parents both gone. She had obviously lost her husband long before she even realized it. And now, now they were trying to take her child away from her, the only thing left in her life.

She rocked and stared at the discoloured area on the wall that had once held a collage of their wedding pictures.

Daddy might not be here, but he had set an example for her of handling things. Daddy would not have sat here wallowing; he'd have acted.

But what action was there to take?

She thought again about grabbing Timothy and fleeing. Maybe she should have done that when the judge first proclaimed the need for a social worker and psychologist interfering in their lives. Look how *that* had worked out.

Rising, she went to her desk for some paper. She remembered daddy talking about making a pros and cons list when faced with a decision.

Sitting at her desk, she folded the paper in half, labeling one column pro and the other con.

Pros:

- If we run, it would be just she and Timothy, no one else to interfere, or to worry about trusting.
- I have enough money in trust funds to support them for the rest of their lives.

- My passport is up to date.
- It wouldn't take long to pack for them.
- I wouldn't have to sit through the endless court trial, listening to the mounting evidence of how her husband, the man who had promised to love and cherish her, had tried to have her killed.
- I would not have to give Timothy over to Dr. Mayberry for a week.
- There were no other relatives who might try to find them.
- There were no close friends the police could badger about where they might be. There were advantages to keeping to oneself.
- We used to do just fine alone, she and Timothy. We don't need anyone else.

Cons:

- Timothy's health. No one knew his medical history like Dr. Muller.
- If we run, I could not have his medical records forwarded to a new neurologist, or their location would be discovered.
- I have no passport for Timothy. Did a child even need one?
- I've heard that to take a child out of the country required written consent from both parents if they were not accompanying the child.
- Would the judge send someone after her to retrieve Timothy?
- How could I access my money without giving away their location?

- When I married Jackson, Daddy had set up my trust funds, so I received so much per month into my personal account. While that was enough for them to travel and manage comfortably in this house that was already paid for, it allowed no access to a larger amount of funds for me to purchase a new home wherever they moved.
- I'm not without skills; I could get a job to support them. But how could I be employed without giving away my identity and location?
- Would we forever be on the run? Did I have enough money for that?
- Is this in my son's best interests? What kind of life would it be for Timothy if we moved every few weeks? What would happen when he needed to start school?
- I could homeschool him. But how could his progress be recorded? What would happen when he wanted to go to college?
- While *I* had think we're fine when it's just the two of them, was I fooling myself? It might have been enough for me, but was it fair to Timothy? Look how he enjoyed playing with Amy and Daniel and even at the birthday party. Maybe he needed more than just his mother. If we were always on the run, how would he make friends?
- Part of cocooning here at home, just the two of us, is the security it gives us. We're safe. If we were constantly looking over our shoulders, on the move, afraid the authorities are coming after us, what kind of security did that afford us?

She sat back and inspected her list. Surely there were more things to add to the pro side. There had to be.

Money was a hold-up. Never in her life had Elizabeth had to worry about finances; money was just always there, in amounts more than adequate for anything that she wanted.

When she turned eighteen, some of her trust funds had opened to her. Daddy guided her in how to make investments that would pay dividends continuously. When she turned twenty-five, she had access to more accounts. This was just before her marriage and daddy had again helped her, taking the time to secure the money for her, making sure it would always be there, he'd said.

It thrilled Jackson that they received this house as a wedding present. He'd been miffed though when he looked at the deed and realized that it registered in her name alone. Daddy explained that that was often the case with women; the home was their security, especially when they didn't have employment outside of the home. He pointed out to Jackson how freeing it was for him to not have a mortgage hanging over his head. Later, if they wanted something bigger, they could sell this place and use the revenue to purchase something else, and the large down payment would reduce the mortgage Jackson would take on. When explained like that, Jackson felt better.

Now, Elizabeth wondered. When her parents died, she learned that their home had been in both mother's and daddy's names. Both of her parents' names were on all their bank and investment accounts. Why did daddy set things up so that Jackson was not included on any of Elizabeth's accounts? Did he know? Did he sense something in Jackson that Elizabeth had failed to see? Surely, if he had guessed all that was about to rain down on Elizabeth, he would have taken steps to protect her. Wouldn't he? Or did he?

Moping wasn't her style. It felt better to be making lists and analyzing possibilities than hugging herself in the recliner.

She started a second paper, this one looking at the pros and cons of complying with the judge.

Pros:

- I'd be obeying the law. I always have, never giving it a thought. It was the right thing to do.
- It would prove my cooperation. Surely, the judge would approve my choices more quickly and leave them alone.
- It showed that I have her son's best interests at heart, no matter how much I would miss him during the week.
- What was a week when they had a lifetime together?
- Maybe Dr. Mayberry was right. Did she see something in Timothy that I, his mother overlooked?
- Maybe Timothy would come back to me a healthier, happier child.
- Although it felt way too soon, within the next year Timothy would be spending longer periods away from me as he started school.
- So far, he'd spent time away from me with Amy and Cynthia, and in the courthouse playroom. He seemed fine after those experiences, maybe even better.
- This was all about Timothy, not about how she, Elizabeth felt.

- Although I'd thought I'd always done my best in caring for my son, look what had happened. He developed a serious seizure disorder. Someone had kidnapped him. His father tried to have his mother killed. Perhaps my judgement was not as sound as I'd believed, and I needed to trust the opinions of others.
- Was it possible that the psychologist saw something in me that was stopping me from being a good mother?
- Dr. Mayberry was my choice. After all that research, I'd felt that Mayberry was the person I'd most trust with my son's care.
- The judge agreed that Dr. Mayberry had a good reputation.

Cons:

- I'd miss my son; I'd miss him tremendously. They'd never spent a night apart since his birth.
- This house would feel so silent and alone with just me in it.
- Do I trust Dr. Mayberry?
- Although Mayberry was tough on me, she'd been only gentle and nurturing with Timothy.

The last time she checked with the lawyer, his advice was to comply with the judge's orders. This time would be no different; how could it be, especially when it was a psychologist of Elizabeth's choosing?

Why did obeying the rules feel so wrong?

Chapter Twenty-Eight

She packed the bag while Timothy napped. She didn't want him to see her tears.

It crossed her mind to pack one for herself as well and just flee with her son. While he could not cross borders without a passport, they could go to another part of the country, one where no one knew them.

But how long could they remain there before Timothy needed his prescription refilled? Or he missed his next appointment with Dr. Muller? She could not risk his health, no matter what it did to her.

Into the suitcase went his favourite pyjamas, toys, and even his Thomas the Tank Engine bed sheets, plate and cereal bowl. He might need all the comforts he could get.

She hadn't told him. On the advice of Dr. Mayberry, they'd tell him together what the coming week had in store for him. Dr. Mayberry assured her that Timothy would take his cue from his mother. If she acted tearful, so would he. If she showed apprehension, he would be frightened. If she made it seem like a fun holiday was in store for him, then likely he would sense that and respond accordingly.

The goal was to make this as painless for Timothy as possible. Her own pain? Well, she'd have to deal with it.

"Walk away."

"What? I can't. He's upset!"

"Walk away," repeated Dr. Mayberry. "There is nothing you can do now to help him. If you linger, it will only make it worse for him. He needs to learn to trust me. You've trained him to allow no one in but you. How's that going to work for him in life?"

Maybe the psychologist had a point, but he was only four. He'd been through so much in these past months; she, his mother, was his only constant. And now, he was crying, sobbing, reaching for her and this woman, this professional who professed to know so much, to know what was best for her son, was telling her to turn her back and walk away from him.

As if on cue, Doris, Dr. Mayberry's receptionist, came into the room. Gently, she took Elizabeth's arm, turned her away from her shrieking child and led her from the room. "It'll be all right. Trust me. Trust Dr. Mayberry. She's excellent with children. She knows what she's doing." Doris repeated this same litany over and over as she led Elizabeth to a seat. "Just sit a minute and get your bearings. Take a deep breath. It'll be all right." She patted Elizabeth's hand and returned in minutes with a steaming cup of tea. "Here, drink. Dr. Mayberry had me prepare some herbal tea for you. It has a calming effect. It's from her own personal collection." She cocked her head. "Listen. Can you hear that his crying has lessened? Now that you're not in the room, he's settling down. I bet that Honey is on his lap. He loves that cat." When Elizabeth didn't reply, she went on, "You are so lucky that Dr. Mayberry is willing to devote this much time to your son. She is wonderful. She is quite taken with your boy. She's cancelled all her other appointments for the next week so she can concentrate just on Timothy."

Elizabeth wished that she felt lucky. She sipped her tea. There was an odd aftertaste, but the spicy, flowery tea was mostly all right. She was more of an Earl Grey or orange pekoe person, but it was kind of Doris and Dr. Mayberry to anticipate that she might want some tea.

After a bit, some of her tension released. It was quiet behind Dr. Mayberry's inner office door. The psychologist was right, and without Elizabeth's presence, Timothy had calmed right down. Perhaps she did project her emotions onto her son. Maybe this would all work out for the better.

When she rose to go, she was a bit wobbly on her feet. Doris urged her to sit down again. "Emotional stress can take a toll on the body, you know. Why don't I call you a cab and you can come back later for your car?"

Elizabeth's limbs felt too heavy for her to bother to protest. It was easier to just go with the flow. In a way, it was nice to have someone look after her.

She shook her head. She never napped during the day, but there she was, asleep on the recliner. The doorbell rang again. That's what must have woken her.

Hoisting herself up was harder than it should be. Geez. What was the matter with her? Doris must have been right about emotional upsets taking a toll on the body. Or maybe she slept in an awkward position.

Elizabeth went to the door, turned the deadbolts, and

pulled. The door wouldn't open. What? She peered closer and realized that she had just slid the deadbolts home, rather than undoing them. She never, ever forgot to fasten the locks when she came in. How could this have happened?

She opened the door. Keira and Daniel smiled at her. How had she not known it was them? Had she really opened the door without first checking the monitors? She gave her head a shake. She needed to get her brain back in the game.

"Hey." Keira gave her a quick hug. As Daniel moved to brush by them, Keira put her hand on her son's shoulder. "What do you say to Elizabeth?"

The child glanced up at Elizabeth, then down at the floor. "Hi."

Elizabeth gave him a quick hug. "Nice to see you, Daniel. Come on in."

Daniel headed for the living room and looked around. Then he headed up the stairs, presumably looking for his friend.

"He's not here," called Elizabeth.

Keira frowned. "Where is he?"

"It's a long story. I'm not sure I want to get into it now."

Then Daniel was in front of her, looking questioningly.

How to explain to a child. "He's away visiting a friend."

"Get him," instructed Daniel.

"Daniel!" Horrified, Keira corrected her son. "That is not how you speak to Elizabeth."

"Please," he corrected. "Get him, please." This was a lot of words for Daniel.

"I'm sorry, sweetie, but I can't. He's gone for a week."

"I thought that you said you have no relatives. No close friends around here." This wasn't making sense to Keira.

Elizabeth was near tears.

Keira held up her hand. "First, is Timothy all right?"

Elizabeth nodded.

"Wait. Wait right here." She led Daniel into the living room to Timothy's toy chest while she pulled her phone from her pocket. "You play here while the grownups talk," she instructed her son. Then, into the phone, "Hey, Jake. Are you free? I need a favor. Can you come to Elizabeth's, pick up Daniel and hang with him for a while?" She listened. "Thanks. See you shortly."

Keira took Elizabeth's arm and led her into the kitchen. She seated Elizabeth, then made herself at home, starting the coffee pot. She sat across the table from her friend. "What's going on?"

Her stiff upper lip seemed to have forsaken her. Tears streamed down her face non-stop as the entire story came out. The judge questioning her decisions as a mother in bringing Timothy to court and keeping him to herself. The home visits and investigation by Anna. The mandated assessment and therapy from a psychologist. How she'd chosen Dr. Mayberry herself. Then the results of Dr. Mayberry's report and how she had to turn Timothy over to the psychologist for a whole week. Maybe even longer.

Some of it, Keira could wrap her mind around. Elizabeth had been pretty uptight and withdrawn when they'd first met, but no one could question her love for her son. Keira was fiercely protective of her child, also; it came with the territory when you were a single mother and had been let down or abandoned by those around you.

Not that she'd had much experience with psychologists, but it seemed strange, the therapist taking the child into her own home for a week. What was up with that?

Jake arrived just as Elizabeth was finishing her story. Keira pulled him into the hallway to give him the shortened version of what was going on. His frown matched hers. "Weird, don't you think?"

He joined the women at the kitchen table. He covered Elizabeth's hand with one of his. "You have friends, you know. We'll help you through this." He didn't say that everything would be all right because something seemed off. His cop instinct reared its head. He'd run this by Brendan. Changing the subject, he said, "I didn't notice your car outside."

"Oh." Elizabeth had forgotten all about that. "I left it at Dr. Mayberry's office and took a cab home. Doris said I should."

"Who's Doris?" This was getting even stranger.

"Dr. Mayberry's secretary. After I drank some tea, it exhausted me. The emotional strain, they said, so it would be best if I didn't drive."

"Where are your keys?"

"In my purse, I think."

Keira brought her her purse.

"Yes, here they are."

"Give them to me, okay? I'll pick up Brendan and we'll bring your car back here." He looked closely at Elizabeth. Her eyes were red and swollen from crying, but there was something else about them that didn't look right. Were her pupils dilated? He rose and said to Keira, "May I take your car? Then I won't have to move Daniel's car seat. I'll leave you mine." To Daniel, he yelled, "Come on, bud. Put the toys away, then you and I are going to hang out at your place for a bit. But maybe we should get some ice cream first."

There was the sound of toys hurriedly being slung into the wooden toy box.

He gave Elizabeth's shoulder's a hug. "We'll figure this out." His look to Keira said that there might be more going on than they knew.

Chapter Twenty-Nine

Keira heated soup and made sandwiches. Elizabeth pushed the soggy croutons around her soup bowl. Keira didn't think that any of the liquid made it into her friend's mouth. She gave up on conversation and left Elizabeth to sit in silence.

The doorbell rang. Keira checked the monitors to see Brendan. Announcing his arrival to Elizabeth, she let him in. He'd brought Elizabeth's car home.

"Liz, Brendan brought your car for you. I'll take Jake's and head on home. Jake will be by later to pick up Brendan."

No response.

"Go on in," Keira told Brendan. Her usual exuberant tone was hushed. "She's in a bad way and could use some cheering up." Then, she added, "Jake wants to talk to you. He thinks there may be more going on than we know." Keira made a quick stop in the living room to give Elizabeth a hug. "See you tomorrow."

Brendan locked up behind Keira, then stood in the doorway watching Elizabeth. She slouched on the sofa, her head back and her eyes closed. Brendan had never seen Elizabeth slouch. She always sat properly, primly even. Her hair looked like she'd run her fingers through it so many times it retained the fingermarks. This usually so-well-groomed woman looked done in.

As Jake and Brendan had driven to pick up Elizabeth's car, Jake filled him in on what had been going on, although they both sensed that they didn't have the full story.

The judge ordering a home study was not that unusual, especially where there'd be a transfer of custody. Having a court psychologist do an assessment was not unusual. Elizabeth admitted that she had requested a psychologist of her choosing, rather than the court's therapist.

Only where the child's safety was in question was the child removed from the home. The child would be placed in a foster home or therapeutic group home. But Brendan and Jake had never heard of a psychologist volunteering to have a child in his or her own home.

Elizabeth was his immediate concern.

He approached the couch and perched on its edge. She didn't move. He took her hand, rubbing it between his, trying to infuse it with some warmth. Where had the strong, independent woman gone, the one like a momma bear with her son? She seemed deflated, as if the life had gone out of her.

With one finger, he brushed errant strands of hair from Elizabeth's forehead. This was the first time he had seen her not fully put-together. Although he did not want her distressed, he also liked this vulnerable, rather messy, more approachable woman.

"Come here," he said. When she didn't resist, he leaned

back, gathered her into his arms and rested his chin on her head. He sat and held her for the next half hour, just held her.

The doorbell rang; Elizabeth didn't move. "That'll be Jake. I'll let him in." He settled her back on the couch. Her eyes were open now.

"Hey, man." Jake clasped Brendan's arm, and then came in, giving Elizabeth a hug. She responded with a squeeze back.

"Do you want me to stay?" offered Brendan. "I can bunk on this couch."

Elizabeth roused and used both hands to push her hair from her face. "No, I'm fine, but thank you anyway. I think I need to be alone." She stood and walked the men to the door. Some of her spunk was returning.

Brendan gave her a lingering hug, his lips lingering near her ear. "I'll see you tomorrow. We'll figure this out, I promise. It'll all be okay."

She nodded. It had to be.

Elizabeth checked again that all the locks were secured, and then wandered around the too silent house. Although Timothy talked little, somehow, he filled the place with his presence. It was an empty shell without him.

Passing by her bathroom, she noticed the almost unused package of lavender bath salts. She rarely had time for a leisurely soak since Timothy came into their lives. She unscrewed the lid. Yes, it still had its calming scent. She turned on the hot water, set the plug, and poured in far more than needed of the salts. Soon the room filled with a wonderful aroma and the water was a pale lilac. Peeling off her clothes, she let them drop where they fell on the floor, the first time in her life she could remember doing that. Lowering herself into the silky water, she smiled at her minor act of defiance - the first time her lips had curved upward all day.

She sat suddenly, sloshing water all over. Who cared? Reaching for a bath sheet, she wrapped it around her and padded to the den. In Jackson's liquor cabinet was some fine scotch. He enjoyed expensive scotch; she rarely had time to imbibe, but now, why not? She half-filled a crystal goblet and sipped. Ah, yes. Smooth. Guess Jackson was good for something. She sank back under the soothing bath water.

Maybe there was something to the whole aromatherapy thing. She felt refreshed after her bath and ready to crawl into bed. She glanced at the jumble of clothing on the bath-room floor and stepped over them. Her mother wasn't here to see. No one was.

She awoke later than usual, surprised that she had slept. Must have been the scotch, or emotional exhaustion from yesterday. Usually, her inner alarm had her out of bed shortly before Timothy would awaken.

She wondered how he had fared in a strange bed. Did he miss her? Was he thinking of her right now?

Out of habit, she went into her son's room; all the toys stowed in their proper places and his bed neatly made with the hospital corners tucked tightly in place. She wandered the room, letting her fingers linger on things that meant a lot to Timothy. Sitting in the rocker, she noticed the head-phones perched on a stand on his bookcase. Maybe listening to the music that flooded his ears so many times a day would help her, as well. The few brief times she'd put them to her ears, she hadn't minded the Gregorian or Mozart music.

Resting her head against the chair's back, she pressed play on the remote and prepared to relax into the music. She rocked in time to the Gregorian chant. Although she was unsure about the science behind this therapy supposedly changing brain waves, it was calming.

Suddenly, Dr. Mayberry's voice filled her ears. She froze mid-rock and listened.

"She tried to hurt you. She let that wicked man take you. He wanted to hurt you and she was going to let him."

What! Elizabeth stood, a hand on either ear, pushing the headphones closer, as if to hear better.

"Soon, soon, you'll come be with me. I will keep you safe. We'll have fun; we'll have a great life together."

Elizabeth's feet took her from the room, downstairs.

"Don't listen to your mother. She doesn't love you. Like your father, she's going away and then we'll have a lovely time together, just you and me."

It went on and on, sometimes the same stuff repeated, sometimes a new variation. Then an interlude of music, then more of her insane directives.

This woman was mad! And she had Timothy!

"Doris? Hello, this is Elizabeth Whitmore. Please give me Dr. Mayberry's address?"

"I'm sorry, but I cannot give out that information to anyone."

"She has my son!"

"Yes, ma'am. I know that that was the plan. She cancelled all her other appointments for this week. You're so lucky that she's willing to devote so much time to your child."

"She's nuts! Do you know what she's been telling my son in those tapes?"

"I'm just the receptionist. I'm not privy to therapy sessions."

"I need that address! I have to go rescue my son."

"I cannot help you with that."

"Give me her phone number, then."

"I can't give that out, either."

Elizabeth hung up. The only time in her life she could recall ending a phone call with someone so abruptly.

She pulled open her desk drawer. Surely, in the invoices she'd signed for their therapy sessions, there was an address, a contact number.

Thankful that she was meticulous in her record-keeping, she opened the file with the invoices. The letterhead gave the office address and phone number. It also gave Dr. Mayberry's registration number with the College of Psychologists.

It took only seconds on the internet to find the local number for the College. Giving the registration number, she requested the phone number and home address for Dr. Mayberry. "I'm sorry, but I cannot give out personal information about our members. Surely, you understand. Not all their clients are stable; it is for everyone's protection that private information remains confidential. I can give you the contact information for her office."

"I *have* that. She took my son! I need to rescue him from her home."

A defensive voice said, "If you have a complaint against one of our members, there are official channels to go through. I can direct you to the page on our website."

For the second time in a half hour, Elizabeth cut off a call.

She could not sit here. She needed to do something, anything, to get her son back. Maybe if she went to the office in person, let Doris listen to the tapes, maybe then she'd give out that address.

Without realizing that she'd not even brushed her hair or her teeth yet this morning, Elizabeth raced upstairs, grabbed the headphones, console and remote, shoved her feet into the first shoes she came across, grabbed her keys, and started the car.

As she backed out of the driveway, she remembered that she'd neglected to set the house alarm, or even lock up. Didn't matter. The enemy was not here; the enemy had her son.

"Ms. Whitmore, I don't really think this is necessary. Whatever is on that tape is confidential, between Dr. Mayberry and her client. It's not my business to listen in on private therapeutic matters."

Ignoring her objections, Elizabeth put the earphones to Doris's head and hit play. For the first half minute Doris looked bored. "Not really my style of music," she said.

Then Doris's eyes widened as the music faded and Dr. Mayberry's words took over. "That's her voice. I know it." She listened some more. "My god, what is she saying?" Doris turned shocked eyes to Elizabeth's. "Why would she be saying such things?"

"Why indeed? There's more," Elizabeth said. "Want to hear the rest? There's over a half hour of this vile stuff, then music, then more. It goes on for hours, getting worse and worse."

"It makes no sense. Why would Dr. Mayberry say such things? And, to a child?"

"I can think of no *good* reason she would force my son to listen to this garbage, but a number of bad, very bad reasons come to mind." She took back the headphones. "*Now* will you give me that home address? You see why I need to go get my son."

"Yes, I understand, but I'm sorry. I can't help you. I don't *know* where she lives. I don't even have her cell phone number." She rummaged in her desk. "Wait! If I ever need to reach her when she'd not in the office, I got through her answering service. It isn't immediate, but they get a message to her, then she calls me back."

"I'll take it." Elizabeth thought a minute. "Please don't call her service. I don't want her to have warning that I'll be coming for Timothy."

As she pushed open the door leading to the parking lot, hurried footsteps followed her. Her brain leapt to the possibility that it was Dr. Mayberry. Of course, it wasn't. Life could not be that easy.

It was Doris. "Ms. Whitmore. I know it's not much help, but Dr. Mayberry doesn't live right in the city. She has a long commute; I think she says that she takes forty-five minutes to get here from her place. And I think she's on a lake or near some water. She talks about sitting on her dock and taking out her kayak." She rubbed her fingers. "I wish I could be of more help."

"You and me both," Elizabeth muttered under her breath.

At least she had a clue now. Not much of one, but she had an approximate radius from the office and the fact that Mayberry's house was on some water. Not that that was much help. There were a lot of natural and man-made bodies of water around the city, both small and large.

Chapter Thirty

Back home, her internet search proved fruitless. Maybe not fruitless if she had a week or two to delve into it, or wait for her requested search through Land Titles, but she didn't have that time. *Timothy* didn't have time. What might that mad woman be saying to him, doing to him?

Much as she valued her independence and desperately wanted to rush to her son's side, she was getting nowhere. She needed help.

"Brendan?"

"Hey, Elizabeth. How did you sleep?"

"I need help."

"Sure, anything. What can I do?"

"I think Dr. Mayberry might be insane and she has Timothy."

Silence. "Could you say that again? What makes you think that your psychologist is insane?"

"The woman is unstable. Can you get over here? I have tapes you should listen to, then you'll get it."

Next, she phoned Keira. "Please, Keira, I hate to ask this of you, but I'm desperate. Could you come here? Without Daniel? I know it's a lot to ask."

"Hold on. Jake's here and he's on the phone with Brendan. He's motioning me to come. Daniel's at school, so I'm free until three."

Jake grabbed Keira's phone and yelled into it, "We're on our way."

Brendan arrived first. Elizabeth was waiting at the door. He wrapped her in his arms. "Whatever it is, we'll fix it."

Elizabeth pulled back. "You can't make a promise like that. You don't even know what's happening."

"We'll fix it, or we'll work on it together." He poked her in the side. "Jake and I are outstanding detectives. We found *you* last time, you'll remember."

"Come here and listen to this." She led Brendan into the living room where she had the headphones on the coffee table. "This is one of the tapes Dr. Mayberry made for Timothy. She insisted that he listen to them a couple of hours a day. The first ones were just music; I checked. But she said she'd be altering them over the weeks, adjusting the tempo and frequency range. I thought that was it, so I didn't listen to every single one. There were hours of them every week." Her shoulders slumped. "Oh, god. Why didn't I check out each one? I was such a trusting fool."

"What are the tapes for?"

"Mayberry said that they're part of Auditory Integration Training and that they'd help Timothy deal with his past trauma and improve his language development."

Brendan fiddled with the headphones, enlarging them to fit over his much larger cranium. "It's just music, old-time music."

"Keep listening." Elizabeth fast-forwarded the tape. She could tell by the expression on Brendan's face when Mayberry's talking overtook the music.

"Son of a ...!" He pulled the headphones off. "She said this garbage to a kid? She's nuts! The whole thing is nuts!"

Pounding came from the front door. "Elizabeth?" yelled Jake.

Brendan opened the door and thrust the headphones at Jake.

"What's this?"

"Just put them on, will ya? Ya don't need to question everything - just do it." Brendan held the headphones so that both Keira and Jake could hear at the same time. "Play it louder," he instructed Elizabeth.

She rewound until she could hear the music come faintly through the headset's speakers.

Jake looked impatiently at his partner. "*This* is what you want me to listen to? It sounds like ancient monks' music."

Keira watched Elizabeth's face and jabbed Jake in the ribs. "Shut up. This is important."

The words were hardly out of her mouth before Mayberry's speech overrode the music. Keira's eyes widened. She clutched Jake's arm, her nails digging in.

Jake's eyes met his partner's. In their line of work, they'd seen crazy. This definitely fell into that class. But this particular crazy had a boy who was close to both of their hearts. "Don't worry," he told Elizabeth. "We've got this. We'll have Timothy back in no time."

Elizabeth didn't look convinced. "How? We need to move NOW!"

In the hallway, Brendan paced with his phone to his ear. "Yeah, make and model. And the address. We need that first."

Jake was there with his pencil and notebook. As Brendan read the address aloud, Jake wrote it down.

"No," said Elizabeth. "That's not it. That's her office's address, not her home. We need to know where she lives."

Brendan was still on the phone. "There's no other address listed for that vehicle? Okay, try the address on her driver's license. We need the home address of Dr. Hanna Mayberry. Check her property records." He listened. "No, I don't have her date of birth. Get that from her driver's license." He paced some more. "Nothing? Just that same office address? Do a background check. Keep on it and get back to me as soon as you can."

"Property records," said Jake. "I'll call." He went into the dining room to make his calls.

Keira hugged Elizabeth. "These guys will figure it out. They're detectives; they're the best. And they love Timothy." She rubbed her friend's back. "Have you had breakfast?"

Elizabeth shook her head. "No, I can't eat."

"I'll make coffee, then."

Brendan and Jake gathered around the kitchen table. "We need to start a Probable Cause," suggested Brendan.

"Yeah. Think we have enough for that. It's just that it takes time." He explained to Keira and Elizabeth. "Paperwork. It's the bane of a cop's life."

Jake got to his feet. "I'll head to the office and get started on the paperwork." He held his mug up. "Got a travel mug I could transfer this to?"

She didn't move or answer his question. "I don't care about protecting Mayberry's rights. I just want my son back." Elizabeth's teeth clenched so hard the cords in her neck stood out.

Chapter Thirty-One

"Jake will find out through NCIC if she's ever done anything like this before." Although, I doubt it, Brendan muttered to himself. "Show me the research you did when you found Mayberry," he said to Elizabeth.

Within seconds, the file folder was in his hands. The web pages she hadn't printed out were listed. "I only printed off the important ones. I don't recall seeing her address on any of them, just her credentials and accolades."

Scanning quickly, Brendan didn't see any indications of where she lived either. Figures. Anyone using their office address for their driver's license probably didn't let such information reach the public.

"We can get the address through her psychology association, but that will take time. Jake's on that." He handed the file back to Elizabeth. Rather than putting it away, she set it on the desk. "Let's head back to her office. Maybe there's something we can find there."

"Hold on," called Elizabeth. "I forgot my phone and I

might need it." She sprinted back into the house, grabbed her phone from the desktop and ran to Brendan's car.

From the back seat of his car, Keira tried calling her neighbor to see if she could pick Daniel up from preschool that afternoon. It looked like she'd be sticking with Elizabeth for a while.

"Sometimes just seeing a badge will make people open up more." That was Brendan's hope, anyway.

A flustered Doris let them into the office.

"How do you pay for office supplies?" asked Brendan.

"We order from this catalog." Doris pulled it from the credenza.

"Can I see some past invoices?" When Doris produced them, he saw that they referenced only this office address. "What do you know about incidentals? Petty cash?"

"We don't have petty cash, but for other things, we have this credit card." She pulled it from the locked file cabinet. Guessing his next request, she pulled the file is this year's credit card statements. Again, it listed just the office address.

"Do you know if the bills have always come to the office? Might they have gone to her home address at some time?"

"I don't know for sure, but I don't think so. We have the last seven year's invoices stored down the hall." She retrieved them. Keira spread them on the credenza and took over the job of checking each one, starting from the oldest. No joy.

"Rent, your cleaning service, things like that. How are they paid?"

"Those things automatically come out of the bank account."

"You wouldn't have those statements, would you?" asked Brendan.

"Here."

They all listed just the office address, even the bank statements. Brendan noted the bank and account number; he'd pursue that avenue later if needed.

"What about in her other office?" Elizabeth pointed at the inner door and headed in. She sat behind the desk and began rifling through the drawers.

Brendan caught her hands. "Anything obtained illegally cannot be used in court. We need to be careful how we proceed."

"I don't care about court. All I care about is getting Timothy back."

Doris shooed Elizabeth out of the chair and plunked herself down. "Let me. I'm supposed to be here, and I can go through this desk." The desk was neat. There wasn't much personal stuff in it.

Keira wandered the room, searching for anything obvious. "What's this door?" It was narrow and painted to blend in with the wall.

"That's Honey's home-away-from-home."

"Honey?"

"Dr. Mayberry's cat. She uses it for therapy."

Keira opened the door. "Wow!" She'd seen climbing structures for cats, but never anything so elaborate. It took up the entire closet space, full of nooks and crannies, open, soft boxes, carpeted climbing poles and assorted perches to delight any feline. "She must love her cat."

Yes! Of course, Dr. Mayberry loved her cat. That meant she must take good care of it. Elizabeth turned to Doris. "Does she take it to the vet?"

"Religiously. They groom her there, too."

"Do you know the vet?"

"I'll get the address and phone number for you."

Looking at the location, Brendan said, "It's close to here. Let's drop in. We might get more in person than from a phone call. It's harder to stonewall when you are face-to-face with someone."

"I'll keep looking through the office," offered Doris.

Showing his badge, Brendan explained, "We're trying to locate Dr. Mayberry. I believe you provide care for her cat, Honey?"

"Oh, yes, Honey. She's a regular here. Such a sweetie; not all cats are easy to groom, you know."

"It's urgent that we find Dr. Mayberry. Do you have her address listed on file?"

"Yes, Detective." Minutes later, she returned. The address she rattled off was for the office.

"Is there nothing else? A different phone number?"

"No, just this one. Why don't I let you talk to our groomer? She spends the most time with Honey and Dr. Mayberry."

Amelia introduced herself. "Honey is the right name for that cat. She is truly sweet and the easiest cat I've even groomed. Dr. Mayberry adores her."

"Does the doctor ever mention anything about her home or where she lives?"

"Not that I can think of. We mostly talk about Honey, but usually she drops her cat off and picks her up later." Then she thought of something. "They have a genuine bond. A Persian like this requires lots of brushing to keep her coat in such great condition. I think that those two spend lots of time together. Dr. Mayberry even had us order in a special feline life jacket so they could go in the kayak together."

Barely controlling her excitement, Elizabeth asked, "Did she say where they kayak?"

Amelia wrinkled her brow. "No, I'm sorry. I can't recall her mentioning the name of a lake or river. Not sure, but I had the feeling that it was close to her house. She said how she'd like to slip down to the dock in the evening and have a paddle, just the two of them."

Discouraged, they headed back to Dr. Mayberry's office. On the way, Elizabeth's phone rang. It was Doris.

"I don't know if this is any help, but I have something you might want to look at," she said.

"Even though I keep all our appointments in an application on my computer and we both have access to it, Dr. Mayberry is old-fashioned. She still likes to keep an appointment book." When Elizabeth reached for it, Doris held firmly with both hands. "I can't let you see it. It's a confidentiality issue; there are names of clients in here."

Elizabeth huffed in frustration.

"But there is something," continued Doris. "Dr. Mayberry also puts her personal appointments in this book, like the cat groomer. She also records appointments with Dr. Murphy. Here." She handed Brendan several sheets of paper. "I photocopied the dates but whited out any patient names."

"Who's Dr. Murphy?"

"He's *her* psychologist." At their puzzled looks, she explained. "Most good psychologists take care of their own mental health. Being at your best for troubled clients can be difficult, so it's prudent to have someone to talk to, someone professional. Dr. Mayberry has been seeing Dr. Murphy for years; he was one of her instructors in college, she said. They're friends. He might know how to find her."

"There're only dates and times here," complained Brendan.

"Here's Dr. Murphy's office address and phone number."

Chapter Thirty-Two

They had less than ten minutes to wait until Dr. Murphy finished with his client. Brendan held out his badge, then introduced Elizabeth and Keira. "Elizabeth and her son are clients of Dr. Hanna Mayberry."

"Recent clients?" A feeling of dread entered Dr. Murphy's bones.

At Elizabeth's nod, he asked, "How old is your son?"

Composing himself, he invited them to sit. Hanna likely had several four-year-olds on her client list and as per protocol, when she saw a child of that age, she would also spend time with his mother. "How may I help you?" And then added, "Within the bounds of confidentiality, of course."

"Please listen to this." She handed the man the headphones and recorder Dr. Mayberry had made.

As soon as the Gregorian music started, Dr. Murphy realized that this was an example of the Auditory Integration Therapy Hanna had said she was trying with a little boy. It had to be the same child; this was not a common approach, and he didn't think that Hanna had used it in years. Decades, maybe.

He moved to take the headphones off. "I cannot comment on the treatment options used by other professionals."

Elizabeth motioned for him to put the set back on. As he drew it closer to his ears, he could hear Hanna's low, soothing voice. What? That was not part of AIT. Then her words registered. All color left his face. His eyes met Brendan's, then Elizabeth's.

Oh, Hanna. What have you done?

Maybe this was just a slip-up and Hanna had mistakenly let loose some of what was in her mind, things she would never say to a child, never say out loud to anyone.

Elizabeth ruined that thought. "It goes on for hours like this. Sometimes it's worse, saying vile things about me and trying to turn my son against me." Her eyes filled. "Who would do such a thing?"

"Ours is a tough profession. It can do things to people."

"Yeah, tell me about it," responded the police detective. "But you don't steal people's kids."

"Have you talked to Dr. Mayberry about this? That's the first step."

Elizabeth shook her head. "We can't find her. We don't know where she is; no one seems to know."

"She's a private person. Many of us need solitude after being immersed in the personal problems of our clients all day."

"I don't care what she does in her off-hours. I just want my son back."

"Where is he?" asked Dr. Murphy, slipping into psychologist role.

"With Dr. Mayberry."

"Sometimes being in an office is not the best atmosphere. Did they go for a walk or to the park?"

"No, she took him!"

That didn't sound like Hanna. "You must have misunderstood."

"She said that she needed him to herself at her home for a week. She wrote that in her report to the judge who decreed that if the specialist deemed that the most therapeutic action, I must comply."

Dr. Murphy's eyes bugged out. He rose. Oh, Hanna! "What! That is most irregular." He paced, muttering to himself. "If she felt that the child was in danger at home, she would have recommended that he be removed and placed in temporary foster care." Turning to Elizabeth, he asked, "Why did you let him go?"

"Because the court said I must, based on Dr. Mayberry's report!" Was the man thick?

"Did you not play this," he pointed to the headset he carried, "to the judge?"

"I didn't know what was on the tapes until this morning. I was missing my son, so sat down to listen to his tapes, trying to feel closer to him. I'd listened to some when Dr. Mayberry first prescribed them, but they were just music. Not until this morning did I, realize the repulsive stuff she was feeding into his head."

"Where are they now?" Perhaps, thought Dr. Murphy, I can help reverse some of this damage.

"We don't KNOW! That's why we're here. No one seems to know where she lives. She said she was taking him to her home, but where's that?"

Brendan's phone rang. He walked to the side of the room to answer it.

"I got it," said Jake. "Here's her address."

At the same time, Dr. Murphy was looking something

up in his book, then scribbling on a piece of paper. "Here," he said. "Here's where she lives."

Brendan read the address into the phone. "Is that a match?" He listened. "Good. Meet you there. We're on our way."

He led the way out the door, Elizabeth and Keira hurrying to keep up, Dr. Murphy on their heels. "Cancel my appointments for the rest of the day," he instructed his receptionist.

Elizabeth halted. "Where are you going?"

"With you."

"But you're her friend."

"Yes, and colleague. But I'm a psychologist first and my ethics take precedence."

Brendan got in his face. "You are not warning her. You are not interfering. The child is our priority. Nothing else matters. Nothing."

"Agreed," said Dr. Murphy. And he meant it.

Chapter Thirty-Three

Elizabeth's phone rang. Thinking it was about Timothy, she put it on speaker phone.

"Elizabeth, this is Anna. I'm here for our scheduled visit. When I knocked, your door pushed open. Your car's in the driveway, so I thought you'd left the front door open for me. But when I went in and called, no one was home."

"Anna, I'm sorry. I totally forgot you were coming. We have a problem - Timothy's missing."

"Missing? I thought this was his week with Dr. Mayberry."

Quickly, Elizabeth filled her in on what was on the tapes the psychologist had forced Timothy to listen to and what seemed to be that woman's intentions.

"I'll let judge Bursey know," Anna said. "Tell me what I can do to help."

Keira interrupted. "Hey, Anna, this is Keira. There is something you could do to help. I'm with Elizabeth and I don't want them to take the time to run me back home. A neighbor is picking up Daniel from school in about fifteen minutes. Could she bring him to you at Elizabeth's house? Would you be able to stay with him?"

"My afternoon is free once I talk to the judge. Sure, have Daniel come over. He knows me. We'll have a good time together."

"Thanks! He loves you. I'll come for him as soon as I can."

Elizabeth hung up and turned to Keira with regret. Here these people were putting their lives on hold to help her and she'd forgotten all about the responsibilities in their lives.

Keira read her mind. "Don't even go there. We've got this covered. Daniel will be there, ready to play with Timothy."

Not wanting to spook the psychologist, Brendan cut his siren about ten blocks before they reached the gated community where Dr. Mayberry's residence overlooked Lake Pleasant. At one time it had been a pond in a farmer's field. Developers took over, widening and deepening the body of water into a recreation area, convenient and private for those willing to pay for the luxury of water in their backyard.

His badge got them in through the gate. He told the guard that the police were on their way and to direct them to Dr. Hanna Mayberry's house.

They pulled up across the road from her place. "Stay here," Brendan told Elizabeth and Keira as he got out of the car. "Wait for Jake."

He'd only taken a few steps when he heard two doors quietly shut. He sighed. Yeah, like that worked. He motioned for the women to keep close to him; obviously, they weren't going to remain in the car. He drew his gun. A noise behind him had him spinning around. A car engine shut off, and another door opened. Dr. Murphy joined them.

"I might be able to help," he said. "She trusts me."

The front of the house showed no sign of life.

"Stay here," instructed Brendan, glaring. "I mean it." He took out his mag light. "I'll be right back." Glancing over his shoulder to reinforce his order, he headed around the side of the house to the right. In seconds he was back, then he tried to other side. Lights shone from there and from the back of the building. He rang the doorbell, wishing he had backup. Where was Jake?

Ah, he recognized the sound of that souped up motor. His partner had arrived.

With a quick kiss to Keira's cheek and a squeeze to Elizabeth's shoulders, nodding toward Murphy, he asked, "Who's this?"

"I'm Dr. Arnold Murphy, Hanna Mayberry's psychologist."

Jake looked him up and down." Good at your job, are ya?"

Keira elbowed him. "Not now," she hissed.

"It's all right. I deserve that and will have lots of time later to ponder my faults. But now, let's get that boy."

"I hear ya." To Brendan, he asked, "Noticed anyone?"

"Nothing, and this door's locked. You stay here with the women. I'll check out the back and let you know what I see."

The plans changed; Elizabeth was already heading around the side of the house.

"Son of a...." muttered Brendan.

Soft music came from the house. Soft lights illuminated the landscaped garden, with sculpted flower beds, seating areas and a brick patio.

Lounging in a cushioned rattan chair, a shoe dangling from one foot, sat Dr. Mayberry, twirling a snifter of amber liquid. Ignoring the rest, she addressed Arnold Murphy. "Et tu, Brute?"

His face reddened.

She laughed. "It's okay. I know what this must be doing to you. All the self-doubt, all the questions and what ifs." She took a sip. "But thank you for the warning call. This might have gone down differently, but for that."

All eyes turned to Murphy.

He held up his hands. "I just asked her where the boy was, pleaded with her to give him up. I tried to tell her that this was madness and would not end well for anyone."

"And?" asked Brendan.

"She laughed. She called me a fool." He looked at the shoe hanging off the end of Mayberry's foot. "She's right."

"Well, this isn't about you," said Jake. "I don't give a shit about you or your feelings. We just want Timothy safe and at home. You can wallow later and psychoanalyze yourself to death."

Elizabeth spoke for the first time in half an hour. "Where is my son?"

"Oh, he's off having a good time. No need to worry about him. He's experiencing things you'd never allow."

Elizabeth's nails bit into her palms. Never a violent person, life had changed her. Now she understood the need to get physical with someone. If she could, she'd drag his whereabouts out of this woman by any means she could. She took a step forward.

Brendan's hand on her arm stopped her. "We'll handle this. It's our job."

Could she trust them to do what was necessary?

"Where is he," demanded Jake.

Dr. Mayberry eyed the weapon held at his side. "Gonna shoot me, are you?" She laughed. "Not sure how that will help you find him."

Murphy sat in the matching chair. "Hanna, for the love of god, where is the child? Turn him over to his mother. Please."

"I don't have him," she replied. "The child is free now." She turned to Elizabeth. "Free in ways that he never could be with you, free to explore and grow and test himself, free from your restrictive reins." She sipped again, inspecting the liquid in the light. "Do you have any idea what you've done to that dear boy? How you stifled his development with your controlling, overprotective ways?"

Elizabeth's throat made a noise. Keira put an arm around her.

"I'm searching inside," Jake told his partner.

"Search away," said Hanna. "He's not there, but feel free to amuse yourself."

"Where is he? Please." Elizabeth would beg if she had to.

Hanna pointed with her glass to the vast expanse of water. "He's free. He's probably having the time of his life right now and you'll never see it, never even know."

247

Chapter Thirty-Four

"He loves being on the water." Dr. Mayberry taunted Elizabeth. "Did you even know that?" Without waiting for an answer, she went on. "No, of course you didn't. You're so wrapped up in your own head, in your own pitiful 'woe is me'. Your world revolves around you, not what's best for that child."

Elizabeth flinched with each verbal attack, each arrow finding its target. No, she had had no idea that Timothy would enjoy swimming; she'd kept him far away from any bodies of water. Look what water had done to her family.

Was that selfish of her? Was the psychologist right that her own fears and experiences prevented her from allowing her son to grow and develop?

Jackson had always complained that she overprotected the boy. But he didn't know the toll that the seizures took on that little body and on her as she watched him go through them. Jackson had never attended a neurologist appointment to view the results of an electroencephalogram, to hear the brain damage that could occur if the seizures continued unchecked. In her research, she'd come across Lennox-Gastaut, a form of epileptic encephalopathy, her worst nightmare. Any parent's nightmare where the abnormal EEG patterns and frequent seizures worsened the child's behavior and lowered his intelligence level. No, that was a fate she didn't see in Timothy's future. She'd do anything she could to prevent his life heading down that path.

Jackson hadn't understood. He ridiculed her efforts to keep Timothy on a ketogenic diet, hoping to lessen the seizures. He'd slip their son forbidden foods. Every time another seizure occurred, he'd mock her, saying this is what their son had become under her care.

Now, Dr. Mayberry was ridiculing her mothering. Two significant adults in her life in agreement about how wrong she did things.

But there was no one else to bounce ideas off, no other concerned adult to discuss parenting issues with. Whose fault was that, a voice in her head questioned? Was it normal to have no friends? Literally *no* friends? She'd felt that Timothy took up all her time, but was that really true? Jackson complained that there was no time for him in her life since they had Timothy. Had she neglected her husband? Is that why he took up with that woman?

She had no objective measure. Wasn't that why they'd been seeing a psychologist to get that outside perspective? No wonder Judge Bursey had ordered these assessments.

But then there was Anna Sanchez. *She* was an impartial outsider sent to evaluate her life, hers and Timothy's. *She* wasn't critical; she was supportive. Maybe, though, that was just Anna; she was that type of person, a social worker at heart.

Elizabeth dragged her mind back into the present, where Brendan and Jake questioned Dr. Mayberry. "Where's Timothy?"

With a smile, Dr. Mayberry turned away, arms crossed, looking out across the water.

Louder, "*Where's* Timothy?"

"He's gone," said Dr. Mayberry, half turning towards them, her smile satisfied. "I tried," she explained. "I would have given him a good life, a chance, opportunities he'd never have had with you."

Jake grabbed both of Mayberry's arms and spun her to face him. "Where. Is. The. Boy?"

Mayberry waved her arm toward the water. "Who knows? Somewhere down there. If I can't have him," her gaze penetrated Elizabeth's, "you won't either."

Her message got through. "Are you saying he's out on the water? Alone?"

That smug smile was back. "He's happy. He likes the kayak. He had a great time out there with me yesterday. I told him he's a big boy now and can go by himself."

"By himself! He's four!"

"Oh, I know he's too small to work the paddle well, so I towed him out with the boat." Her eyes had a nasty glint. "When I last saw him, he was smiling. 'Big boy', he said."

Keira rummaged in her oversized shoulder bag. She pulled out a pair of binoculars; Daniel loved to look through them. Holding them to her eyes, she scanned the horizon, sweeping right to left, then back again. "There!" She pointed. "There. I see an orange kayak!" She passed the glasses to Jake.

"She's right." Then, to Dr. Mayberry, "How do we get out there?"

"Oh, you can't, not unless you're a superb swimmer."

"How did you tow him out that far?"

Mayberry pointed to where something shimmered not far offshore. "With that. When I got back, I unscrewed the plug on the bottom of the boat. It didn't take long to sink."

Brendan was already charging through the house, out the sliding glass doors at the back. Elizabeth was on his heels as they ran down the sloping lawn to the dock.

"Jake, do you think we can raise the boat?" As Brendan got closer, he saw it was a lost cause. Possible, but it would take equipment and hours. They didn't have hours. He threw off his jacket as he ran, balancing on first one foot, then the other as he tossed off his shoes. "Here," he said to Jake, handing over his weapons. As Jake prepared to remove his clothes to join him, he yelled, "No. Guard Mayberry. Call for backup. Get the paramedics here."

The splash he heard was Elizabeth diving into the water, her shoes and coat in a pile on the dock. "Wait, Elizabeth. It's a long way out there."

She didn't respond, just worked at her steady crawl. It had been years since she had swum, years since she had ventured into the water, years since that day that her brother died. He died because of her. That would not happen to Timothy.

Brendan overtook her, his stroke more practiced, more powerful. He used enough breath to tell her, "We'll get him. Don't worry." They were only about a quarter of the way to the kayak, but the tiny boat was getting bigger. "He's fine. The boat isn't rocking; he won't fall out. We can take it easy getting there." He did not want to have to rescue them both.

Elizabeth didn't reply, just concentrated on her breathing and her strokes, her eyes never leaving that bright, orange plastic kayak.

She slowed. Sucking in precious air, she yelled, "Timothy!" Did the tiny boat wobble? Oh, she shouldn't have called to him. A wee, small body lifted itself upright. Maybe he'd been sleeping, and she woke him up. "Sit still, son. We're coming!" Please don't move around, please sit right still.

With everything in her, she willed her limbs to move again, to keep going. Although her muscle memory recalled how to move in the water, those same muscles weakened from lack of use. Never again would she be a couch potato. Breathe, breathe, she told herself. She closed her eyes, orienting herself by the sounds Brendan made as he swam beside her, keeping pace. No, she didn't need that. As much as she wanted to be the one to rescue her son, she needed help. "Go," she told Brendan. "You can get to him faster. I'm all right. Go to him."

Brendan left her side, slowly pulling ahead, with several glances back at her.

Timothy was more important than her pride. She could trust this man to get her son.

Chapter Thirty-Five

"Hey, bud," he called softly. Now that he was beside the kayak, he didn't want to startle the child or do anything to cause him to fall into the chilly water.

The kayak wobbled as Timothy spun around at the words. Brendan put out a hand to steady it, even as he tried to calm his own breathing.

"Bren!" replied Timothy. "See me? I sail." The child's face showed dried tear streaks.

"That you are, buddy." Gently, he turned the hull of the kayak, aiming it back toward shore. He pointed. "See? In the water there? That's your mom, coming to see you. Let's go meet her." Pushing the kayak from its stern, he said, "Hang on to the sides."

It felt like hours, but in minutes, Elizabeth met the kayak.

"Mommy! You camed!" Timothy leaned over to hug her.

"No, son, later. Sit up straight. Don't want to tip out."

"Why don't you get up on there with him?"

"No, you can push faster without my weight." Tempting as it was to hold her Timothy in her arms, this wasn't about her. She clung to the side with her left hand resting beside her son's. With her other arm and both legs, she helped propel them forward.

Elizabeth shut her eyes, praying that she could keep going. Never, ever was she letting herself get this out of shape again. She wasn't fat by any means, but geez, where was her strength, her stamina?

Trusting Brendan to steer them to the dock, she concentrated on moving her legs and her arm, murmuring reassuring words to Timothy.

The child whimpered and put both his hands on her arm, but didn't panic or thrash. Could a four-year-old know what he had to do to keep safe?

"Give me your arms," instructed Jake. Heedless of the wet, he hoisted Elizabeth out of the water. She collapsed on the dock, but only for a few seconds. The bumping sound told her that the kayak was here. "Timothy," she called. Keira wrapped her coat around Elizabeth's shivering shoulders.

"I've got him," said Jake. He trussed the boy up in Brendan's jacket, folding it around the small boy several times. He placed the sausage-shaped Timothy into his mother's arms. Next, he gave his friend a hand up, hauling him up onto the dock.

Jake placed another coat over his friend's shoulders.

Brendan crouched over the mother and child, scanning the landscape, searching for anything else that might threaten these two who were coming to mean so much to him.

Jake stood beside them, weapon pointing down at his side, watching the officers load Hanna Mayberry into the back of the squad car.

The psychologist's eyes pierced the group huddled at the end of the dock. Her gaze spoke volumes of hate for those who had thwarted her plans.

Anna agreed with Dr. Murphy. Don't strangle Timothy. But Elizabeth found it almost impossible to not keep her arms around him. Her boy would tolerate it for a certain amount of time, then he'd squirm to get free.

Although it was hard to take the advice of someone who had been Dr. Mayberry's friend, Elizabeth tried to see Dr. Murphy as another victim. Even he, a trained professional, was deceived by Dr. Mayberry, not realizing what she was capable of. How an experienced psychologist couldn't see through the woman's front was beyond her, though.

Anna explained that Dr. Mayberry was good. Her training taught her to conceal her actual feelings, and put on the front that her clients needed. Putting up that facade was second nature after all these years, and she'd perfected it. When he was with her, Dr. Murphy dropped his psychologist-patient role and simply saw a colleague, a friend. Now, he was paying for his lapse; his remorse ran deep, and he'd apologized over and over and over for not have seen what was going on, for not having stopped the abduction.

For that's what it was, an abduction. That's how the prosecution saw it. Dr. Mayberry remained in custody, awaiting arraignment.

Judge Bursey apologized. It didn't sit well with him, but he did it anyway. Although, obliquely, he held Elizabeth equally responsible since she was the one who chose Dr. Mayberry.

His original ruling held, though. Timothy must be evaluated by a psychologist, in addition to the social worker's assessment. This time, Elizabeth agreed to involvement from the court-appointed psychologist, Dr. Henry Henderson. He seemed to have no hard feelings that Elizabeth had passed him by the first time.

"You did what you felt you needed to do," he told her. "I understand. So much of your world was out of your control that you were trying to exert your authority in whatever ways you could."

Relieved that he wasn't angry or insulted, Elizabeth apologized again.

"Not necessary," he told her. "We're good. If you want me to work with Timothy and you, I will."

Chapter Thirty-Six

Timothy planted himself in his favorite spot on the kitchen floor, spinning pot lids with precision. Elizabeth reached into the drawer for another one, attempting to mimic her son's skill. The lid did a nice rotation once, twice, then teetered to one side before crashing to the floor.

He laughed, meeting her eyes, sharing his glee. "Like this," Timothy said, demonstrating how to put the proper spin on the lid.

Elizabeth tried again, this time reaching for one of her son's perfectly balanced lids. He didn't mind that she interrupted its spin but laughed at her efforts. She reached for him, dragging him onto her lap and tickling. His kicking legs sent all the pot lids flying. Didn't matter. They were together and having fun.

The doorbell rang. Timothy ran to the monitors. "It's Anna," he yelled. He raced to the door and opened the bottom two locks. He had to wait for Elizabeth to reach the top one for him. Soon, he'd think to drag over a chair to take care of that one himself. She had some rules to teach before that time came.

"Anna!" Timothy yelled, throwing himself into her arms. She picked him up for a hug and spun him around. In a short time, this woman had become a friend. Elizabeth wondered at how easily Timothy trusted her. Maybe he was a better judge of people than was his mother.

She gave Anna a hug. Funny, she'd never been a hugger before this. But now she understood why people did it.

A knock at the door. Through the peephole, Elizabeth saw Brendan. Opening to him, she went into his arms, breathing in his scent and leaning on his broad chest.

There was a tug on Brendan's pant leg. He released Elizabeth to throw Timothy into the air, then over his back for a piggyback ride. It had become their thing, a ritual every time Brendan entered the door, which was often these days. "Don't shut the door," he told her. "Jake and crew are pulling into the driveway just behind me."

"Daniel!" yelled Timothy. Then the two boys were off, up to Timothy's room.

Keira and Jake entered, their arms full of boxes and aromas. Jake complained about how much he had to carry since Brendan had set his contribution on the porch steps, so he could put his arms around Elizabeth.

Not long after, the bell rang again.

Elizabeth hollered up the stairs, "Timothy, Amy's here." She hollered, actually hollered. Her mother's face would show distaste if she were here. Elizabeth smiled at the thought.

Timothy and Daniel pelted down the stairs to grab Amy and then raced back to their games. Things were louder up there now, with the addition of Amy.

Cynthia wrapped her arms around Elizabeth and gave a tight squeeze. She had become a friend. Cynthia greeted the others and the noise volume in the once quiet house grew.

As the wine flowed and the appetizers vanished from the serving plates, the bell rang a last time. On the other side of the screen was an uncomfortable-looking Dr. Arnold Murphy asking, "Are you sure you want me here?"

"Of course." Elizabeth pulled him inside. The man had done everything he could to atone for missing the fact that Hanna Mayberry was losing it. He offered to assist Dr. Henderson, the court psychologist, with any insights into the things Mayberry might have said to Timothy.

Elizabeth noticed his eyes light up when he spied Anna.

There was a time when Elizabeth prided herself on her tidy, serene home, with everything in its proper place. Now, her living area was a mess. But it was a good mess. The three kids played underfoot, with toys strewn all over. The adults scattered their belongings as well, with wine glasses, plates, and napkins on most flat surfaces. Once, this would have bothered Elizabeth.

Funny how it seemed all right this evening. She had friends who would help her clean up. But that was for later. Now, she would just relax and enjoy the noisy companionship of these people who had become her friends. People who didn't care that her hair had come loose from its usually sleek chignon, who didn't care that the canapés were slightly burnt around the edges.

How could she have thought that she was fine alone, just her and Timothy? In protecting her son, she had been unable to do it alone. It was okay to lean on others. She liked these people and trusted them. While others had let her down, not everyone was like that. Rather than trying to *take* her life, there were people willing to defend her life with their own.

Since she had let others into her world, life felt richer. It all came down to one five-letter, ever so fragile word - trust. Trust with others and in herself.

Next in the When Bad Things Happen series

vinci-books.com/SELFISH

A mysterious child, a shadowed history, and a woman's quest for redemption.

In the somber halls of the courthouse, a silent child wanders, her presence a riddle that entwines her fate with Anna's in unexpected ways. As Anna embraces the responsibility of caring for this enigmatic girl, shadows from her own past begin to stir, threatening to unravel the life she has painstakingly built.

Turn the page for a free preview…

SELFISH: Chapter One

"I never want to see the inside of a courtroom again. Ever!"

"Well, hello to you, too, Elizabeth."

"I'm sorry, Anna. Your door was open, so I just walked in and started at you. That's not like me."

"A lot that's happened to you lately isn't like you."

"Or the me I ever wanted to be. Growing up, I was a goody-goody, always the rule-follower, never making waves. And yeah, look what that got me." She grimaced. "But not everything that happened was bad. I met you." She walked around Anna's desk to give the woman a hug. "Who'd have thought that being kidnapped and my husband trying to kill me, would bring me friends I never knew I needed. For you, I might consider stepping foot inside this courthouse." She thought for a second. "Unless you're about to move your office to a better location?"

"Being a court-appointed social worker pretty much means that I hang out here."

"How'd the pre-sentencing go?"

"Dr. Mayberry won't be seeing daylight for a long time. Judge Bursey was not pleased with her. She not only took us all for a ride, she made him look foolish for having approved of her." She twisted her hands together. "But at least she didn't get Timothy."

"How is your little man?"

Elizabeth brightened. "He's great! He seems less traumatized by all that happened than I am. Maybe it's the resiliency of youth, or maybe," she regarded Anna from the corner of her eye, "it's your Dr. Murphy working his magic."

Anna blushed. "He's not my anything."

"That's not the sense I get from him."

"We're friends."

"No, Murph and I have become friends. He does not look at me in the same way he looks at you."

"Knock, knock," came a deeper voice from the doorway. Both women jumped as he continued. "Anna, you should close your door if you don't want people walking in on you."

"Hey, Murph," said Elizabeth. "We were just talking about you."

He raised an eyebrow; his steady gaze rested on Anna's blush. "Hopefully nothing bad."

Anna's hair partially hid her face, but she was smiling. Arnold Murphy pushed off from the doorjamb and strode to Anna to give her a kiss on the cheek, then did the same to Elizabeth, but this one was briefer, as he asked, "Are you joining us for lunch?"

"Lunch?" Elizabeth looked from Murph to Anna.

Behind Murph's back, Anna nodded her head vigorously. Her eyes said, "Please" even before her lips did.

Grinning, Elizabeth pretended to consider. "Thanks, but I'd better get home. It was rough sitting in that courtroom all day and I need to get in a workout before I pick up Timothy."

"If you're sure…" said Murph.

"We'd love to have you come with us…" said Anna at the same time.

"If I didn't have a healthy ego, Elizabeth, I'd swear that she'd rather have lunch with you than with me," said Murph. His twinkle told Elizabeth that he'd picked up on Anna's nervousness. "She's a hard one to pin down, although I think I'm growing on her."

"Hellooo, I'm right here," interrupted Anna.

"And I'm not," said Elizabeth, "or I won't be in a minute." She gathered her purse and phone. "See you later and have a nice lunch date."

"It's not a…" started Anna.

"We will," said Murph.

He waited while Anna finished up the email she'd been working on, then set her phone to take messages.

"Shall we?" He held out his elbow to Anna.

She'd have to be rude to not take his arm. But in some ways, even though the contact flustered her, it was easier than looking him in the eye. They had to walk right through the reception area where the secretary sat and past the other social workers. Anna was positive that Murph knew this and had her on his arm on purpose.

"Did Elizabeth tell you about the pre-sentencing hearing this morning?"

"Just a bit," answered Anna. "She didn't think Hanna would get out for a long time."

"Probably true. But I don't know. Elizabeth might have put her own spin on things." Murph picked up his menu. "This was an attempted abduction. Timothy's mother willingly handed the child to Hanna, and Hanna had a judge's approval for the plan. But it was her intention to keep the boy. And the prosecution argued that she meant the boy harm by pushing him out on the lake in a boat by himself. I don't know how much time she'll actually get."

"She tried to steal Timothy!"

"You and I know that. I testified to her worsening mental health."

Before Anna could interrupt, he added, "Yes, I know. It wasn't my fault, and she showed her 'together' side to me, but I'm a psychiatrist. I should have seen through her. I was growing concerned but had no idea she was that far gone."

"She's clever," said Anna. "And she knew just what to say to you."

"Yes, she is clever. That's what worries me. She will know how to play the system. Whatever her sentence, I'm positive she'll be released early. She'll know all the right things to say and do."

"At least Timothy's safe."

"Yes, and so will other children be safe from her. She'll not be allowed to practice child psychology ever again."

"I can't bear anyone harming a child."

Murph wrapped his hands around hers. "Now, let's talk about something more pleasant."

Anna relaxed.

"When are you going to agree to move in with me?"

One year ago in Tijuana, Mexico

Turning into a side street, Evaline leaned her back against the cracking concrete wall. Taking a deep breath, she listened carefully, then stuck as little of her face as she could around the corner, checking that no one followed.

No, no one.

Bending her knees, she let her back slide down the wall, scraping away some flaking paint as she did so. Sitting on the sidewalk, she brought her knees up to her stomach. They didn't come as close as they once had; the bulge of her stomach held them off. She rubbed a hand over her belly.

How had this happened? Well, she knew how. She even knew when. What she didn't know was how she had let herself get into this predicament.

She thought Cal loved her. Yeah, he loved to get into her was about it. It had only been a couple of times, but that was enough to cause this.

She hid it for a while. The puking was only for a few hours each morning, and since she was the only one up at that time, it was not hard to hide her nausea. Not that anyone would notice if she was pale. She could continue at her job. The money certainly was not great, but enough to help her family, plus give her a bit to spend.

Then her mother noticed her bulge. They were alone, just the two of them that afternoon. Her madre had pulled up Evaline's shirt and then shrieked. A torrent of words came out, but all Evaline heard was shame and sin.

When her padre came home from the cantina that night, there was more hollering. Then a beating. Then nothing. Exactly nothing more for Evaline. They'd kicked her out for shaming the family. That was it. No clothes, no money, no place to stay.

The first few places Evaline tried to find to sleep didn't work for long. Dogs found her and were suspicious that she was a rival for the food they scrounged by the dumpsters. She spent much of that first night walking, keeping to the shadows, leery of strangers who might come across her in the night.

SELFISH: Chapter Two

There. Anna thought she spied her again. Although not rare, it wasn't that common to see children in the courthouse. Sadly, sometimes their family circumstances brought them here. But to see a child wandering the halls alone was not the norm.

Although not positive, Anna thought she had noticed this young girl earlier in the day, not just once but possibly several times. She was always alone, always walking and watching, but never seeming attached to any of the staff or clients who had reason to be in the building. Now, it was nearing the end of office hours and the building would shut down soon.

Grabbing an empty coffee cup, Anna set out on a path to intersect the girl. She looked to be around twelve or so, a pre-teen or early adolescent, anyway. The child looked more nervous than she had earlier in the day.

"Hey there, hi," she said. "I'm about to get some hot chocolate. Want some?"

The girl didn't reply, but her eyes said what her words

didn't. She looked longingly at Anna's cup, making Anna wonder when the child's last meal had been.

"Our break room's just up here. Come on and I'll get you some." She didn't turn her head, hoping that the girl would follow her. She did.

"I'm Anna," she offered.

The girl didn't speak.

Not usually one for small talk, Anna chatted away about nothing, wanting to put the child at ease.

As the TASSIMO machine churned out the first cup of hot chocolate, Anna passed the mug to the girl. The child's hands trembled slightly as she took the mug. Low blood sugar from not eating? Either that, or she was extremely shy.

The girl downed half her drink before Anna's brewed. Immediately, Anna started a third cup coming. Once ready, she swapped it out for the empty mug the child clutched. "One's never enough for me," she said.

The child sipped this one more slowly as Anna rummaged in the cupboards for some cookies, anything to fill the hole in this little girl's stomach.

She gestured toward the table and pulled out a chair for herself. Elbows on the table, Anna tried to portray as much nonchalance as possible. She heard another chair scraping on the floor tiles as the child sat down.

"My name's Anna." She held out her hand.

The child set her cup carefully on the table and took her hand in a quick, tepid, shake.

"What's your name?"

No response.

To fill the silence, Anna made some inane comments about the cookies they were consuming, how she preferred the brand with more chocolate chips in them, or at least the oatmeal/raisin kind.

"Are your parents with you?"

Nothing

"Did you get lost?"

No response.

"Is someone coming for you? Are you supposed to meet them?"

The girl shuffled, then pushed back her chair.

Worried that she was about to bolt, Anna feigned an enormous yawn. "Goodness, this has been a long day, hasn't it? I'm beat. Some days are like that, you know." From the corner of her eye, she watched the girl's shoulders relax, just slightly.

"Tomlins will be happy to see me. He's my cat, you know. Do you have a cat?"

The girl shook her head.

"Want to see a picture of him?"

Anna wasn't sure, but the child might have inched a little closer. Pulling out her wallet, Anna showed her pictures of her beloved cat, a twenty-pound tabby who loved his kibble and treats. It showed.

Yes, she hadn't imagined it. The girl leaned closer. Anna handed her the case that held the photos, pointing out various features as the girl shuffled through the pictures. At one photo of the cat sprawled on his back, luxuriating in the sun, the girl gave a half-smile. Almost.

Putting her arm under the table, Anna gave a surreptitious glance at her watch. The offices closed in half an hour, as did the main desk at Child Protective Services.

"The cleaners will be here any minute to start work on

this room. Why don't we take our hot chocolates back to my office? We can finish them there in peace." Again, she rose, hoping that the child would follow. The sound of the chair legs scraping on the floor told her she was.

Keeping up her chatter, they made their way back to Anna's office. Passing through the reception area, Anna made eye contact with the receptionist, trying to convey without words that something was going on. Betty nodded she got it. There was a real plus to working closely together with a team. As she turned the corner to her office, Anna saw Betty heading into the door of their supervisor's room. Good to have a team behind her.

Anna pointed to the couch, telling the girl that it was much more comfortable than the hard wooden chair by her desk. Plus, it was far from the door in case the girl wanted to run. Once the child sat, Anna said she'd be with her in just a couple of minutes; she had a few messages she needed to return, then she could relax with her hot chocolate. First, though, she pulled from her bottom left drawer, a package of crackers. "Want some?"

She picked up her phone. "Hi, Betty. Could you get CPS on the line, please? Tell them to hold and make sure that someone's around. Thanks." Anna logged in to her computer. She turned her chair, so that she was sideways to both the girl on the couch and her desk. She angled her computer monitor so that she could still work, yet the girl could not see the screen. She pulled up her email program and sent a message to Betty saying that she'd noticed this young girl several times since that morning. She was always wandering the hallways alone and didn't seem connected to anyone. So far, the child had not responded to questions, or said a word. Anna wondered if she was a runaway or abandoned? Had someone reported a child as missing? Had there been any family court hearings involving a twelve-year-old girl?

Anna knew Betty would take the message to their supervisor. Surely this girl belonged to someone who must be frantic with worry about what had become of her.

As Anna sipped her now-cooling hot chocolate, she watched the girl. She devoured a dozen crackers in short order, but the two cups of hot chocolate plus the cookies and crackers seemed to have taken off some of the desperate edge. Still, the child did not seem disposed to conversation. She listened, though.

So Anna prattled. She was not skilled at small talk at the best of times, and no one would call her gabby, but her chatter seemed to calm the child. Maybe if she relaxed some, she'd be willing to give up her name, her story, and where she was from. Surely someone was frantic about her disappearance by now.

Or maybe she was hiding here, just as frantic to not be found. In that case, Child Protective Services was definitely needed.

About fifteen minutes later there was a quiet knock on the door. Betty poked her head in and said, "Anna, CPS is here. It's Jillian."

Thank goodness. Jillian was great. "Come on in. Hey, Jillian. How are you?"

"Great, thanks." She turned towards the child on the couch. "And who's this?"

"I'm not sure of her name, but we met in the hallway here and have shared some hot chocolate." She grimaced. "And some stale crackers."

"At this time of day, I'm on board with any kind of

snack." She put her hand toward the box on the couch. "May I?" she asked the girl. Without waiting for an answer, she planted herself on the couch and reached for the box. "Ah, Ritz. And not the low sodium kind, either. Excellent choice." She grinned at the girl as if the child had made the best decision in buying this type.

There was a half-smile, but not much more in response.

Trying a more direct approach, Jillian said, "So, where are you off to when these offices close for the day?"

The child blanched. Maybe she hadn't thought that far ahead.

"Are you here with someone?" She popped more crackers into her mouth and chewed for a few moments. "Anna, do you have a pen and pad of paper we can use, please?"

With these implements on the couch between them, Jillian suggested the girl might be more comfortable writing answers than saying them.

The child made no move to reach for the pen.

"Is someone coming to pick you up?"

No response, no eye contact.

"Can you tell us where you live?"

Nothing.

"Anna, would you please tell Betty to get things moving?" They had a plan in wait.

There was movement in the hallway as staff packed up and shut their doors for the night, ready to head home.

"Bonnie. May I call you Bonnie/" Jillian said to the girl. "I've always liked the name Bonnie and you really seem like a Bonnie lass."

The child's eyes remained glued to the hands in her lap that she twisted and untwisted into knots.

"Bonnie, you can't stay here. You know that, don't you?"

Her warm eyes urged the child to trust her, to talk to her. "Don't worry. We'll find a safe place for you to spend the night." She waited. Nothing. "Is that what you want?"

A gentle tap on the door and two women entered.

"Bonnie, these are my colleagues, Hillary and Pam. They run a receiving home. It's a safe place for you to spend the night. They'll take care of you."

The child raised her wide eyes to Anna's. A film of tears covered them.

Anna went to her and squeezed her hands. "It'll be all right. You'll be safe with these women; they'll take care of you. They've had lots of experience with kids."

The child's eyes never left hers.

"And I'll come see you tomorrow." Now, where did that come from?

Grab your copy...
vinci-books.com/SELFISH

About the Author

Sharon A. Mitchell lives on a farm, with her nearest neighbor several miles away. Does that seem like a setting to spark the imagination? It does for her.

When she's not writing her numerous thriller series, she can be found taking long walks with her hundred-pound German Shepherd dogs, Pickles and Dill. (She didn't name them - don't blame her.)